Praise for *Never Lasting*

"A steamy romance that I devoured in a single sitting and an authentic, bittersweet depiction of how it feels to reconcile big dreams with big love."

—Ilana Wolpert, *Anyone but You* screenwriter

"*Never Lasting* packs an impressive emotional punch—hopeful, heart-aching, and sexy in equal measure. I'll be ready for whatever Bourassa writes next."

—Tarah DeWitt, bestselling author of *Lost and Found* and *Funny Feelings*

Never Lasting

ANGELA BOURASSA

831 STORIES

831 Stories

An imprint of Authors Equity
1123 Broadway, Suite 1008
New York, New York 10010

Cover design by C47
Book design by Scribe Inc.

Library of Congress Control Number: 2026943719
Print ISBN 9798893312195
Ebook ISBN 9798893312218

Printed in the United States of America
First printing

www.831stories.com
www.authorsequity.com

To my husband.

You're really good at sex.

1

LUCY

"This is so embarrassing!" That's what I try to say between sobs in the NYU Law Library bathroom, but there's too much snot, too many mascara-black tears to get the words out.

Rebecca gets the message just the same, but the random graduation attendees unfortunate enough to find themselves in this particular restroom at this particular moment do *not*. Stealing covert glances at me as they wash their hands, they seem torn between calling for medical help and alerting campus security. "Don't worry about them," Rebecca insists, not caring if they hear. "You take your time."

Mortification finally wins out over my primal need for release, and I manage to find my breath while the onlookers skitter out the door. As soon as there's room to spare in my lungs, I blurt out, "I'm so sorry."

"Don't be!" Rebecca offers up half a roll of paper towels, and I can tell she's barely resisting the urge to wipe my face for me. "Of *course* you have big feelings."

That elicits a dark laugh as I bury my face in rough brown paper. "What am I, a toddler?"

"Hey. Big girls have big feelings too."

She reaches toward me, and I let myself sink into a warm, enveloping hug. I'm so done with these tears, this humiliating total fall-apart. My pounding heart starts slowly settling back into place. "God, I look like shit," I half moan, half laugh as I catch my reflection in the mirror. "Guess there's no point crying about it."

Rebecca grabs more paper towels as I turn on the tap and splash my face. I imagine the cold water rushing through my veins, resetting my whole nervous system. Through deep, even breaths, I try to think back to the single tear I shed when the dean handed me my law degree an hour ago. That was the start of this whole downward spiral.

But now, finally on the other side, I feel somehow both lighter and more grounded. Oddly revitalized.

Or maybe I'm just dehydrated.

Judging by the crease between her brows, Rebecca doesn't seem so sure the storm has passed. "I don't think I've ever seen you cry like that."

"I don't think I ever *have* cried like that."

"Not even when . . . ?"

I shake my head. My mom was sick for two years and lost all quality of life months before she passed. It was horrible. Completely awful in every way. But I also felt a sense of relief when her suffering was finally over. In the three years since her death, I have held it together. Weird things—like hearing a song she always sang the wrong lyrics to—will catch me off guard. But I'm usually able to push the tears aside quickly.

Not today.

I catch Rebecca searching my face, wanting to help and not knowing how. But I'm not sure how to explain the intensity of the emotions that have coursed through me for the last hour. I couldn't begin to express myself without losing it again. "I just wish she was here" is all I say.

Rebecca pulls me in for another hug. When our bodies separate, I clasp her hands.

OK. Big, cleansing breath. I watch Rebecca's chest rise and fall in time with me. "Do you have any makeup?" I ask, taking care to steady my voice.

Rebecca pulls a travel-size mascara out of her bag. "Sure you're ready for it?"

I nod. "No more tears. Go see your family. I'll come find you."

"No, I can wait—"

"Go. Be merry." I lean in to remind Rebecca—and myself—of our absurd and amazing accomplishment, the thing we were celebrating before this sob fest: "We're fucking *lawyers.*"

Rebecca chuckles and tilts her head to the side. "Kinda. Not really 'til we pass the bar—"

"No excuses. I'll be right out. Promise."

JAMES

Rebecca may be my favorite cousin, but there's something torturous about graduations—they're somehow always too hot and too long, and this crowd feels particularly suffocating, which is saying something in Manhattan. Maybe it's because so many of these families aren't from here. I've only been in the city a few weeks, but I've noticed that the places where tourists gather are the most overwhelming, even when they aren't the busiest. Locals know how to swim around one another like fish in a pond. Tourists don't swim—they do cannonballs. I hate that I'm currently one of them.

I try to kill time, distracting myself by admiring the swaying tulip trees around Washington Square Park and picking out graduates in the crowd, wondering about their lives.

"What are *you* looking at?" The mock-accusing voice could only be Rebecca.

"I'm trying to figure out which of your classmates are going to be, you know, environmental lawyers and civil rights attorneys—"

"And which ones will help massive companies destroy the fabric of society?"

"Yup, that." I give her a hug. "Congratulations. I'm really proud of you."

Rebecca beams. "Thank you. I'm proud of me too. Now, where the hell are my parents?"

I nod over my shoulder. My aunt and uncle round a

corner, their arms overflowing with plates of cookies, cheese cubes, and mini sandwiches, as if the ceremony was the opening act for the snack spread. Rebecca and I repress our grins as we hurry to help with the haul.

"There's our lawyer!" Aunt June exclaims, dropping an Oreo in the process. Uncle Steve offloads three plates and two cups of lemonade onto me so he can give his daughter a bear hug. I struggle to balance a grape rolling perilously close to its doom.

And that's when I see her.

She's tall, almost as tall as I am, her billowing graduation robe unable to conceal her statuesque frame. Caramel hair falls in soft waves down her back. And her *eyes*. They're nearly black, perfectly offset by her amber skin.

She's scanning the crowd, and as I stare at her, unable to look away, I realize I've seen her before. It's Rebecca's best friend. What was her name? We've never met, but I've heard so many stories about this ride-or-die who Rebecca's always trying to bring on family vacations, but she never comes. I can't remember why.

During the ceremony, she stood next to Rebecca in the crowd of baby lawyers all lined up on the stadium floor as June, Steve, and I looked down from the cheap seats. She was too far away then to make out any distinct features, but I could tell she was wiping tears. That's standard for graduations, right? But there's no trace of those tears now.

There's something, though. Something beyond her appearance. As she searches for familiar faces, she doesn't seem lost or alone. She seems almost *defiant.* The slight curl of her full lips, the way she stands, shoulders back and confident. I'm fully convinced this woman could destroy the fabric of society if she wanted to. I hope she doesn't.

I can't look away.

"Lucy." That's her name. I blurt it out the moment I remember, and her shining eyes find mine, making my stomach clench. She starts striding my way, her lips parting into a curious, playful grin.

"You must be James." Shit, even her voice is amazing. Low, buttery. I momentarily lose all sense of cool as she comes closer.

But then Rebecca spots Lucy and rushes to hug her. "There you are! Wow, you look *amazing.*"

Lucy laughs. "Thanks. I kind of weirdly *feel* amazing? And lots of other things."

"I get that," Rebecca responds, pulling Lucy into a small circle with her parents and me. I realize I'm still staring and force my eyes down to my plate of toothpicked cheese.

"Is this the famous Lucy? Congratulations, sweetie! Your mom would be so proud! Have a lemonade! You look beautiful." Aunt June spews all this so fast that I almost miss that bit about her mom.

Lucy seems unsure how to respond for a split second. "Thank you," she says, deftly covering all the bases.

Rebecca introduces Lucy to her parents, who both forgo handshakes for hugs. Then Rebecca turns to me. "And this is my cousin, James. He's a chef—"

"Cook," I correct her too quickly—and then mentally kick myself for doing so.

Rebecca must clock the flustered look on my face, because she gives her most cunning, catlike smile and immediately dives into my full résumé. "He grew up playing soccer and was pretty talented. He got third place in our sixth-grade spelling bee after me and Celine Yamamoto. He's a big doodler, and weirdly good at it. He likes musicals—"

"OK," I cut in. "Are you done embarrassing me?"

"What's embarrassing?" Lucy asks, a twinkle in her dark eyes. "I love musicals. What are your favorites?"

I feel my ears turn red as I rack my brain. "Uh, *Les Mis. Rocky Horror. Singin' in the Rain. Hello, Dolly!* is hard to beat. What about you?"

Lucy beams back at me for a few seconds before I realize she's teasing me. I chuckle and try not to think about what shade of scarlet my ears must be by now, but then her palm is on my forearm. "I'm sorry." She laughs. "I honestly haven't seen many musicals. Maybe they're not as bad as everyone says."

She pulls her hand away, but the lingering warmth of her skin on mine makes me feel like I could leap a building. "Don't believe the lies," I insist. "Musicals make life worth living."

She laughs again, and I catch the quick look she shoots Rebecca—who has gotten pulled into a side conversation with her parents—and pray it's a good sign. "It was really nice of you to come," Lucy says, and I give a little shrug. "Graduations are so boring, and it's *always* too hot. Actually . . ." She leans close to whisper our first secret: "I almost skipped it myself, honestly."

"I'm glad you didn't," I whisper back, and Lucy's eyes flick up to meet mine, studying me with a sharp curiosity. For a moment, I forget to breathe.

Then she politely turns her attention back to the wider group as Aunt June loads her up with extra mini sandwiches. "You all are quite the refreshment experts."

"Well, James landed us this amazing reservation at Nouveau Riche, but it's not for two more hours," Uncle Steve clarifies between sugar cookie bites.

Rebecca leans close to her mom, lowering her voice. "Did you manage to . . . ?" She gives a subtle nod in the direction of Lucy that Lucy pretends not to notice, though I spot the slight pink in her cheeks.

"I'm sorry, honey. We tried, but the restaurant couldn't make room for one more." Aunt June turns to Lucy with a pitying look. "But maybe you could join us for a drink?"

Rebecca looks like she might crawl up inside herself and die, but Lucy just stands up straighter. "Oh, I have plans. A lot of the international students don't have family here, so they invited me to join their party." A somewhat awkward silence falls. "I hear there's going to be a taco truck!" she adds.

She says it with such forced excitement, I have to stifle a laugh, and Lucy elbows me in the rib. It's the kind of thing an old friend would do, and I shift my weight toward her, leaning into the familiarity.

"Well, it was so nice to meet you all," Lucy announces, passing her untouched plate to me but stealing back an Oreo for the road. "Enjoy your dinner!"

Wait, she's leaving? Lucy gives Rebecca a tight hug, and I watch them exchange whispers, Rebecca clearly trying to get her to stay. But Lucy seems determined. I watch in a small panic as Lucy smiles at Rebecca, then at me, and strides away.

"Lucy!" As I hurry to catch her, she stops and turns back, and I'm completely unsure what I can or should say. I just know I don't want her to walk away.

Lucy waits, watching me with a steadily furrowing brow as I search for the right words. "Have dinner with me," I finally manage.

The corner of her mouth curls upward, but her brow remains crinkled. "Aren't you the one who landed the swanky reservation?"

"Yes." I've actually been looking forward to this meal all week—Nouveau Riche's lamb piccata is the stuff of legends. But I'd eat sand for the chance to keep talking to Lucy. "Turns out, they only have space for three. You know, one of those classic fine-dining . . . three-top tables."

Lucy's cheeks glow. "Right. Classic. For all the throuples."

"Exactly. Very *nouveau*."

"Very."

Our eyes linger on each other. I fight not to look at her collarbone, the hint of skin peeking out of her robe. "So you see," I say, mustering what I hope comes across as charm, “I could really use a dinner companion. You’d be doing me a favor.”

I watch Lucy’s eyes dart to Rebecca, checking via best-friend telepathy whether this is OK. I don’t dare look at Rebecca myself.

When Lucy’s eyes return to mine, her cheeks glow a shade rosier. “Where to?”

11

LUCY

In the bathroom after Rebecca left, part of me wanted to sink back into my tears. To sneak off to my bedroom and spend the rest of the night with takeout dumplings and the *Gilmore Girls*.

But I'm so glad the other part of me won out. The part that recognized I have achieved something consequential, something that deserves to be celebrated. The part that said my mom would want me to be happy today. To be proud. To be unstoppable.

And I don't really believe in signs from the universe, but something about the way James called out my name felt . . . momentous.

I'd seen pictures of him, heard about him for years. But I wasn't prepared for the impression he makes in person. He's tall—taller than me—and broad. I sneak a glance at his face as we walk down the sidewalks of the Village in charged silence. He seems a bit nervous, which only makes him more attractive. And the freckles that speckle his cheeks and nose give him a boyish charm that's pretty irresistible.

It was the way he looked at me, though, when we met. The way he gave me his full attention. The way he didn't let me run away. I was so grateful for my graduation robe in that moment—it concealed the distinct shiver running up my spine.

Our first stop was the administration building to turn in my gown, and now I'm in my favorite summer dress—a knee-length, flowy red number with cap sleeves and a sweetheart neckline. Knowing I'd be on my feet for hours at graduation, I went with flat strappy sandals, and now I see James is in sandals of his own—a bold choice in a city where everyone has oddly strong opinions about exposed male feet.

"You have nice toes," I say, causing James to peer down.

"You're into feet?"

"Let's not reveal our kinks just yet."

I want to backtrack the moment the words leave my lips, but James laughs. "Right. I think the revealing of fetishes traditionally falls on date six."

He's funny. Why didn't I tag along on one of Rebecca's family vacations when I had the chance? "So this is a date? Not just, I don't know, pity?"

"You're taking pity on me?" he asks.

"No, I—"

James laughs again, and I feel a rush of warmth in my chest. In the back of my mind, I'd been rehashing that joke I made about musicals earlier, wondering if I overstepped, but now it's clear he likes teasing too.

He turns to look me in the eye as we continue down Bowery, and I drink in those adorable freckles. There's one centered perfectly under his left eye that I'm particularly enamored with. "This is a date." He says it definitively. No playful tone this time.

I have to take a moment to make sure my voice won't shake before speaking again. "Good."

"But," James adds, "there's a caveat." He runs a hand through his close-cropped sandy-blond hair. He suddenly seems more nervous, which makes me nervous. *What is it?* A dozen possibilities flash through my mind in the split second before James continues, "I'm only in New York for the summer."

"Oh." The lump in my throat immediately dissolves.

"I'm moving home to Oregon. To open my own restaurant."

I forgot that he cooks. "That's amazing!"

"It is?"

"I mean, yeah. Congratulations."

"Thanks." James rubs his neck, still uncertain. "I just figured I should tell you now . . ."

It clicks—he was worried about leading me on. "How very thoughtful of you," I say, bumping his elbow with mine. "I guess now would be a good time to tell you I'm also leaving soon. In six weeks, I head to The Hague."

James nods slowly. "I'm gonna pretend like I know where that is," he whispers.

My heart swells. *So* many people over the last few months have acted like they knew exactly what I was talking about when they clearly had no idea. "It's in the Netherlands."

"Oh, wow. You're fancy."

"Oregon is fancy too. In a natural-wonder sort of way."

"Good point. We're basically the same."

I laugh. "So the caveat is . . ." I have to tease, "that you won't be proposing tonight?"

James raises his face to the sky, as if graciously taking that hit on the chin. "I just figured it would be the gentlemanly thing to tell you."

"No, you're right. Very gentlemanly." I realize I'm walking a bit serpentine, enjoying the chatter of the strangers we pass and the pepperoni scent wafting out of slice shops. I'm not sure if it's James or my crying jag or graduation—or some combination of all three—but I feel *great.* Like I've been let out of a cage. And I decide to lean into it. "I guess I just take the general viewpoint that all dating in your twenties is temporary."

James raises an eyebrow. "A hater of musicals *and* romance?"

I laugh. "Seriously, though. We're too young for anything real. We've got to figure out who we are and set up the lives we want for ourselves before bringing anyone else into the picture."

"That's fair." He nods. "It would be a lot easier to make a life with someone once I'm settled and have my business running—assuming it doesn't immediately fail."

"Exactly. The making-a-relationship-work part, not the failure part," I clarify.

"OK. No romance for you then." He says it in a matter-of-fact way that makes me practically snort.

"Where are we going on this doomed date, then?" I

ask as we wait at a crosswalk. "And please don't say anywhere as nice as the place you picked for Rebecca. I can't afford that shit."

James chuckles. "No, no, no. I've got a *much* more celebratory spot in mind. And it's about as cheap as it gets."

"Should I be scared?"

He points a block down the street. "That depends. How good is your trash talk?"

JAMES

I don't know anything about this city beyond my tiny world of food friends, so I desperately googled options while Lucy was returning her graduation robe, hoping to find a gold mine within walking distance.

The bowling alley I've led us to is dark and musty, drenched in the scent of multiple decades' worth of cigarettes, oiled wood, and fried food. There are only six lanes, four of which are occupied by a large group of Armenian men, all seemingly sixty and over, all clad in league shirts that read "Jesus Bowls Me Over."

I steal a glance at Lucy as we walk in and the full scene hits her, completely aware that many women would not choose this as the destination for a first date or a graduation celebration. I know I've taken a risk, but Lucy seems like someone who'd prefer an adventure over anything by the book. I brace for potential disaster, but she looks at me with wide eyes. "This is fucking amazing," she whispers.

I don't know if it's this girl or this night, but it's starting to feel like I can do no wrong. My confidence level is dangerously high, and I don't hate the feeling. "Do you bowl?"

"Not at all. Do you?"

"Nope." I grin. "Shall we?"

A few minutes later, we're set up on the far lane with a pitcher of PBR, and we're modeling our matching neon-pink socks and clownish bowling shoes for each other. We opt out of the bumper rails and agree within a few frames what a terrible mistake we made. Almost every ball we roll ineptly down the lane ends up in the gutters, and we mercilessly taunt one another.

"Good thing you have that law degree to fall back on," I tease in the second frame.

"Do you like living in the gutter? Is it cozy?" she counters on my next attempt.

But as much as we savage each other's failures, we cheer wildly for each rare success. Whether I knock down one pin or Lucy knocks down six, we act like we both just won gold in the Olympics, jumping up and down like maniacs, making up victory dances. Our antics draw more than a few raised eyebrows from the gentlemen at the other end of the alley.

Let them stare.

LUCY

As we begin the eighth frame, I realize I've never felt this comfortable with a guy on a first date. Maybe not even a second or third. There's something so goofy about James, so unafraid of looking foolish. And he *does* look foolish, but that doesn't make him any less attractive. Honestly, it's the opposite. His lack of inhibition, the amount of fun he seems to be having with me and—I hope—because of me, is infectious. He may not look his sexiest when he's doing the Electric Slide after knocking down two pins, but right after—*that's* the magic moment. When his face is lit up, he's not at all embarrassed, and he strides over to sit next to me, his muscular arm falling effortlessly around my shoulders. That's the moment when his playfulness becomes an intense turn-on. He isn't afraid, and he's *fun*. I never realized how much I'd been missing that from previous dates. Ridiculous, flirtatious, uninhibited fun.

And I've been acting as silly as he has, busting moves I've never displayed outside my bedroom. The endorphin rush I felt after my sob fest a few hours ago has only intensified. It's like I'm riding this wave of catharsis, and I don't want it to stop.

JAMES

A tiny voice in my head is nagging me to tone it down. *This is the limit*, it says. *You're about to cross into the land of* "*ick.*" But another slightly louder voice keeps urging me on, reminding me, *The clock is ticking with this girl. What is there to lose?* So I keep choosing to trust that louder voice. And each time, Lucy rewards me with a beautiful, full-body laugh. Head tilted back, hair bouncing, her hands landing on my back, my chest, my wrist. She isn't holding back, and neither will I.

We each have truly pathetic scores in the forties as Lucy stands for her final frame. Her first attempt veers into the gutter almost immediately. She turns to me, defiant. "I'm pretty sure that ball is lopsided."

"Mmm. It's practically an egg."

Lucy picks up a new ball for her second go. She gets set and takes a deep breath, holding the glittery purple orb close to her face. Then with just *terrible* form, she sends the ball down the lane. It drifts within an inch of the gutter, but the spin she somehow managed to put on it pulls it back to center. All ten pins go flying.

We stand flat-footed in disbelief for a solid three seconds. Then I let out an involuntary "Woo!" Lucy turns around, and her entire face glows.

I bound to her, picking her up in a spin before I even realize I'm doing it. My hands feel at home on her ribs, just below her breasts. Her palms press into my shoulders as she laughs. "I got a fucking strike!"

"You got a fucking strike!" I set her back down, a little embarrassed to have done something so bold, but she doesn't take her hands off my shoulders, so I cautiously let my palms settle onto her hips, trying to focus on the feeling of the soft cotton of her dress and not her body underneath. "Sorry. I shouldn't have—"

LUCY

Before he can apologize, I spring forward and press my lips to his. It's impulsive and brash and not fully in line with my consent training, but I feel a thousand percent certain James won't mind. After a split second of surprise, his lips press firmly into mine, and he wraps his thick arms tightly around my waist, grasping a section of my hair in his hand. I feel the slight tug through my entire body. The tip of his tongue finds the tip of mine, and we both tilt our heads left in perfect sync, as if this were our thousandth kiss and not our first.

My heart pounds, and my hips greedily push into his. I feel a pulse through his jeans, and maybe noticing, he takes a step back with a boyish grin of embarrassment.

As our lips part, our eyes lock. He seems just as lost for words as I am.

Then the quiet is broken by a grizzled old man at the end of the alley yelling, "It's about damn time!" All the bowlers begin cheering for us, and James and I burst into laughter. He tosses the men a little wave, and I give them a dramatically deep bow.

As I wipe my eyes for the umpteenth time today, I notice the scoreboard. "Oh shit. I guess that was technically a spare."

James leans in for another kiss. "Let's not be technical."

III

LUCY

After we turn in our bowling shoes, we realize how hungry we are. The greasy food options at the alley sound disgusting, but somehow the equally greasy menu at the twenty-four-hour diner down the block sounds amazing.

I sit in a booth across from James, a pair of Cokes between us, the backs of my knees sticking to burgundy vinyl, and I wonder how my day took this turn.

"Can I ask . . ." James takes a moment, sipping his soda before continuing. "My aunt mentioned your mom. Is she . . . ?"

I was hoping to avoid any sort of real talk with him.

I plaster on the sympathetic smile I've perfected over the last three years. The one that says, *Yes, my mom is dead, but you don't have to feel bad about it.* "She died about a month before I started law school. Cervical cancer."

"That's terrible. I'm so sorry."

I start to give my follow-up smile, the one that says, *It's cool. I'm appropriately sad. You're appropriately sad. Let's move on.*

But there's something in his tone that stops me. It's a sincerity that manages to cut through my cynicism, right to my heart—which seems to be beating on the outside of my chest tonight.

"Thank you. I really missed her today."

"Is that why you were crying during the ceremony?"

My eyes dart up to his. "You saw that?"

He winces a little, like he's been caught. "You were next to Rebecca. I couldn't tell who you were or anything. But yeah, I may have noticed a tear or two."

I smirk. "I'm going to choose to find that cute rather than creepy."

James chuckles. "What's creepy about noticing that a fellow human is crying?"

"I don't know, but something definitely is." He laughs with soda in his mouth, struggling to hold it in. It softens me even further. "I was having a lot of big feelings, as Rebecca put it. And they only got bigger as the ceremony went on."

"Oh, yeah?"

I fiddle with my menu, really not wanting to fall back into that emotional pit. "I basically had a full-on meltdown in the bathroom afterward. A couple minutes before you and I met, I was crying maybe the hardest I've ever cried in my life." I sound more flippant than I intend to.

"Wow."

He doesn't seem quite sure what to say next, and it makes my heart clench. I'm not big on sharing my feelings, and definitely not on a first date. I attempt to take a super chill, deeply unaffected sip of my drink and shift the tone back to safe terrain. "Sorry, I don't know why I told you that—"

"No." He covers my hand with his as he says it, catching me off guard. It's like a reflex, as if he can't help physically reaching out to me. "I'm glad you did. I just . . . I don't know, I was trying to imagine what not having your mom today—let alone the last few years—must have felt like." He pauses, his blue-gray eyes locked on mine. "I'm really sorry."

How does he do that? There's no irony in his words, no reservation. His genuine care feels like a warm blanket wrapped around my shoulders. I'm still not sure if I should open up, but my heart acts faster than my head, pulling all the jumbled emotions from this afternoon to the forefront of my mind. I couldn't—or didn't want to—find the words earlier with Rebecca, but they come tumbling out of me now.

"People have this habit of saying stuff like 'It'll get easier with time' or 'Time heals all wounds,'" I mumble. "It's bullshit. Time makes it harder, not easier." His gaze is consistent, all too easy to confide in. "She'd been sick for a few years when she passed. By the end she wasn't able to walk on her own, barely able to talk. I knew I needed to let her go. That she was gone before she actually died." I feel my grief like a knot in my chest, slowly rising up my throat. "But *now* . . . it's like, she's missed so many things. Birthdays and Christmases. Movie nights and long phone calls." Anger swells behind my eyes, and I resist the urge to cry. "I'm mad I didn't get to share today with her. I'm mad she won't be able to visit me in the Netherlands." Glimpses of future memories that will never happen—my mom and I scouring used bookstores, hiking the Hague Forest, inventing backstories for tourists on the beach—bring me a sort of tortured joy. I have to grin as a tear escapes my eye. "We would have had so much fun."

James offers me a melancholy smile. I wonder if he's lost someone too. He seems to understand the mixture of nostalgia and heartbreak flowing through me. Or maybe he's just that empathic. "It was just the two of you?" he asks gently.

I nod, feeling the grip of my emotions loosen, now that I've exposed them so flagrantly. "Always. She wasn't seeing anyone in particular when she got pregnant with me." I smirk. "I remember her telling me when I was six or seven that half a dozen guys could be my father, and she didn't remember the names of any of them."

James chuckles. "That's pretty badass."

I like him more by the second.

"What was she like?" he asks.

"She was funny. Quick. Really kind, but also firm. She took no shit." James scans my face, as if deciding which of these traits I've inherited. "She was a makeup artist," I go on. "Like, a world-class one."

"World-class, huh?"

I nod, pride overtaking me. "She would get booked for magazine shoots and fashion weeks all over the world, and she always brought me with her. We traveled to something like thirty-five countries together. I lost the exact count."

"Holy shit, that's amazing. But how'd that work with school and stuff?"

I grin. "Not very well. I had a combo of homeschooling and bad tutors. I'd go to the local schools whenever we had a few months at our home base—this crappy little apartment outside of Boston—but I managed. Got my GED when I was sixteen, and then I traveled with her for another year before applying to college."

James raises a playful eyebrow. "And what was that like, being stuck in one place for four years?"

I laugh—he's already got me figured out. "I did two different study abroad programs. One in Cairo, one in Munich."

James shakes his head at me, delight painted in his eyes. "Lucy, Lucy, Lucy . . ."

"What?"

"You're just . . . waaay too cool for me."

I laugh so hard that a middle-aged couple bickering over their omelets turns and stares.

"Just, *so far* out of my league," he adds, not letting up. "It's comical, really."

I shake my head. "I assure you, I'm *not* cool."

"Lies."

"I'm not!"

"Then tell me something uncool about yourself."

I shift in my seat as I think, wondering what level of honest to be here.

"See, you can't even think of anything," he says.

"I'm broke?" I say it more like a question than a statement because I'm pretty sure he's not the kind of guy to find this uncool.

James shakes his head again, that perfect freckle under his eye teasing me. "We're in our twenties. Who isn't broke? Besides, aren't you about to become a very well-paid lawyer?"

"Not yet. The thing I'm leaving for in six weeks is a clerkship at the UN International Court of Justice."

"That sounds legit."

"It is. Very prestigious. But it's also ten months of not getting paid."

"Not even a stipend?"

"Nothing." My head tilts involuntarily from side to side—as if trying to hold the anxiety at bay. "Usually your law school covers the cost, but my school has no funding for it this year. I'm actually TA-ing an undergrad summer session—a poli-sci class—so I can earn some extra cash and hold on to my graduate housing until I leave. The big thing I need, though, is this grant for young lawyers in international law. It would cover all my expenses." I lean in, fully giving up on hiding any of my feelings at this point. "I'm honestly not sure what I'll do if I don't get it. My advisor says I'm a shoo-in, but it's still pretty fucking terrifying. *And* on top of that, I've got to study for the bar." I lift up a hand to measure a level high above my head. "My stress level is somewhere around . . . here."

James eyes my hand, then lifts his own fingers to mine,

as if to check my measurement. His polo sleeve slides up and reveals his bicep in the process. "I've seen worse." We share a grin. "When do you find out if you got it?"

"I turn in my application in two weeks, should hear back in four."

"Well," James says, his voice dropping an octave as he picks up his half-empty Coke. "I will help by covering this extravagant dinner."

I normally wouldn't let a guy pay for the first date. I have a thing about it—feels like it sets up an uneven power dynamic. But somehow that's nowhere close to a concern here. "I accept." I pick up my glass and clink it with his.

"So that's your field, international law? Or is this clerkship a résumé-building thing?"

"No, that's the field, a thousand percent. With the way I grew up, it's hard to imagine a different kind of life." I pause, wary of coming across as overly ambitious or arrogant, but James grins at me with a magical, raw sincerity that erases any fear. "I want to go on being a citizen of the world and hopefully leave some kind of positive mark. Maybe make this place a little more just, a little more open."

His eyes catch on my lips before he responds. "Sounds like a good life."

We're both quiet for a moment, and my mind wanders back to our make-out session. Was that really only thirty minutes ago? The memory of his mouth on mine, his fingertips grazing the side of my breast . . .

As he turns his attention to the menu—the first time

he's looked over the options since we got here—I imagine taking his hand under the table, guiding it up my leg, under my dress, and pressing his palm against me. I picture the look we'd share as he pushed my underwear to the side, both trying to keep straight faces, not calling attention to ourselves, as he brought me to a silent, lip-bitten climax.

Then a harried, no-nonsense waiter saunters up to our table, pouring cold water on my daydream.

The waiter doesn't bother asking what we want but instead just stares at us, no pad or pen in sight. "Cheeseburger and fries, no pickle, please," I say. Then I look to James, but he's not looking at the waiter—he's looking at me.

"What would your mom order?"

The question nearly knocks the wind out of me, and I feel my jaw go slack. But I know the answer instantly. "French dip. Extra au jus," I manage to murmur.

James looks at the waiter. "Two of those, please." Then he turns back to me. "Enough to share."

Did he know how much that small gesture would mean? Could he possibly? I can almost feel my heart reach out to his. It's frightening and electric, overwhelming and inevitable. *I could really fall for—*

No.

I stop short. *Don't even think it.*

IV

JAMES

After we order, Lucy gives me a little head shake. "I've been talking too much. Tell me about you," she says. She folds her hands in front of her, and I can almost physically feel the vibe shift, but I'm not sure why.

I try not to dwell on it. "What do you want to know?"

"Everything?" She must see the flash of fear in my eyes, because she quickly recalibrates. "Let's start with this restaurant of yours in Oregon."

"*Proposed* restaurant. I'm not sure I'll be able to make it happen."

"Not with an attitude like that." She gives me a cheesy fake smile. "But why Oregon? Didn't you just get to New York?"

I nod, far from excited to now be the center of the conversation, but at least this is something I know how to talk about. "This is just a stopover. I went to culinary school in Philly and worked at a restaurant there for the last five-ish years. That was great, but they made some changes recently and I ended up . . ."

Lucy offers a kind smile. "Going a different direction?"

I wasn't *exactly* let go, but I might as well have been, so rather than get into the details, I move on. "A friend of mine who's the chef for a catering company offered me a spot here for the summer. It's the busy season, so." I shrug. "I appreciate the work, and the money, but New York isn't really my scene."

Lucy sips her Coke and waits for me to continue. It's simultaneously nerve-racking and a rush to have her full attention on me.

"Back in Oregon, my parents and Rebecca's parents still live on the same street. And my grandma—not the one I share with Rebecca, my other one—her house is just a few blocks away. She watched me all the time. Rebecca, too, and some neighbor kids that I still keep in touch with. It was like one big extended family." I run a hand through my hair, involuntarily remembering how my grandma used to ruffle it. "The plan has always been to go back home. It's my favorite place in the world."

As those words leave my mouth, I'm suddenly aware just how little of the world I've seen, especially in comparison to Lucy. But it's hard to imagine finding another place I love as much.

"Have you actually saved enough to open your own place?" she asks.

"Oh, not even close." She laughs. "But my grandma passed away last year, and she left me her house."

Lucy seems unsure how to respond. "I'm sorry . . . and congrats?"

I hurry to put her at ease. "She was ninety-five, died in her sleep. I miss her, but she lived a great life." A memory warms my chest. "She went on a three-mile walk the day before she died, just like every other day. She'd steal a flower from each neighbor, coming home with a huge bouquet."

Lucy gives me a bittersweet smile. I run a finger over a crack in the vinyl seat.

"Newport—that's the town in Oregon—it's this old seaside village with a wooden boardwalk and unreasonable quantities of chowder. It has *lighthouses*, it's so fucking quaint," I say, and Lucy snort-laughs. "Not a lot of restaurant jobs, but I've always wanted my own place. I'm looking at possible locations and trying to get a loan using the house as collateral." I shrug involuntarily. "I really don't know if it'll work, but I'm trying."

"Why wouldn't it work?" She says it like it's already a done deal, like she has zero doubts I can make this happen. Her confidence in me makes my heart pound.

"I need a *big* loan, and I'm not exactly a Michelin-starred chef."

"You're not? I thought they handed those things out like candy." Her eyes shine, and we share a smirk.

"I just want to make comfort food for regular people. Nothing too elaborate. The dream is a locally loved haunt that flies under the radar, barely pays my bills, and lets me live out my life in my favorite place with my favorite people."

Lucy beams at that, and it's impossible not to beam back at her. "So that's the plan," she murmurs. "When the summer's done, you go to Oregon. Forever."

"That's it."

As the words leave my mouth, my ex-girlfriend's face flashes across my mind—hazel eyes, dimpled cheeks, cropped auburn hair that she tucked behind her ears whenever she laughed.

Miriam and I dated for most of high school and broke up a year into culinary school. The distance was too much for us, and there wasn't a clear end in sight. Miriam is still in Newport as far as I know, and I think she's single—I don't ask our mutual friends, and they don't offer. When I think about moving back, I think of her.

I wonder if I should say any of this to Lucy. If the way she reacted to my admission about leaving New York soon is any indicator, she won't feel threatened or disappointed. But a lot has happened since the beginning of the night.

For now, I choose silence.

Our food arrives, and Lucy chuckles to herself. "What?" I ask.

She pushes the burger she ordered aside and goes for one of the French dips. "It's just funny," she muses as her eyes run over the sandwich fondly. "You're heading to one side of the planet to put down roots, and I'm heading to the other side to go gallivanting from place to place."

"Good use of 'gallivanting.'"

"Thank you."

I rearrange my sandwich with a bit more care than whoever first assembled it. "I guess it is funny. When I said this couldn't go anywhere earlier—"

"You really meant it." She's clearly delighted by the dark humor of it all. Then she sits forward in her seat and grips her sandwich with both hands before lifting her eyes to mine. "Thank you for this. Truly."

We both dip into the au jus and take a big bite. The thinly sliced roast beef and soft buttered roll mixed with steaming broth—no cheese, no nothing—are such a simple, remarkable pleasure.

The conversation dies down as we eat, both quietly savoring. It almost feels ceremonial. Like we're honoring Lucy's mom through beef and bread. I've always had a deep respect for the way food brings people together, the intense meaning that it can hold, but even I didn't anticipate this outcome when I placed the order.

I steal a glance at her, her focus still fully on her sandwich. She either hasn't noticed or doesn't care that her dress has slipped a few inches down her right shoulder, revealing a white satin bra strap. I can't stop myself from following the line of it down her chest to its vanishing point beneath the low cut of her neckline. I trace the tops of her small breasts with my eyes and get lost in a vision of standing behind her, holding her long body against mine. I feel myself start to get hard imagining what her nipples might look like.

She's coming to the end of the first half of her sandwich, and she's really going for it. I watch as she takes a particularly large bite and broth drips down her chin. I did not expect that to make me even harder.

I take a sip of my drink to cool off as she laughs at herself and wipes her chin with the back of her wrist. Her black eyes meet mine, and I feel like I've been caught. But I also sort of hope she senses where my mind is at, what being around her is doing to me.

And maybe she does. Her laughter fades away, but her focus stays on me. Her eyes gain a coyness I remember from the bowling alley. She had that same look after our kiss. "Eat fast," she says. "There's somewhere I want to take you."

V

LUCY

I walk us back in the direction of campus, the streets of the East Village humming with people hustling everywhere and nowhere. I wonder if any of them are having a night like mine.

"Where exactly are you taking me?" James asks, leaning toward me. Maybe he's right about New York not being the right fit for him: He's too hulking for the sidewalks.

"You'll see."

"You're not planning to rob and kill me, right? I have location sharing on."

"Well, there goes that plan."

We share a mischievous grin, and I feel the pad of his middle finger slide down the inside of my palm. My body pulses as his fingers intertwine with mine. "Is this OK?" he asks, meeting my eye.

"Your hands are even nicer than your feet."

He laughs. I caught him by surprise with that one. "And here I thought we weren't going to talk kinks tonight."

We arrive at a campus building with just a few safety

lights on, and I swipe us inside with my student ID. James narrows his eyes, trying to figure out where we're going, but he doesn't ask questions. He lets me have my surprise.

The hallway off the main entrance is dark and empty, lined with large, framed pieces of contemporary art. At the end of the hall is a set of double doors. I get out a key I stuffed in my wallet a few nights ago, the one my adjunct art professor friend gave me to lock up with when he got too drunk at his own exhibit and had to leave early. He probably didn't intend for me to use it for this, but he also didn't drop by my place yesterday to get the key back like he promised he would, so here I am.

James widens his eyes at me as I unlock the door, and I have to grin at his confusion. "Trust me," I tell him, and we step inside. As I let the doors close behind us, we're shrouded in darkness, odd shapes stretching through the shadows all around.

Then I find the panel of light switches and flip them on one by one.

The three-story-tall room comes to life in a golden haze. A massive tree made of crepe paper and copper-wire lights looms over us, its branches reaching out toward countless smaller art projects. They're all calling out to be walked through or played with or even sat on. All glowing with vibrant neon, warm filaments, or carefully sculpted strings of light. Plugs and cords weave in intricate patterns, becoming part of the display. Each piece feels somehow both mechanical and ethereal, thoughtfully constructed and impossible to dissect.

I was blown away by the space when I first saw it a few days ago, but being here alone with James is another feeling entirely. Like this whole night, it feels magical.

I turn back toward him, hoping he sees it the same way I do, and his mouth hangs open as he gapes about. When his eyes land on mine, he strides over to me, takes my face in his hands, and kisses me, pressing his body to mine with an urgency that makes my knees go weak. His tongue finds mine and I melt into him.

I reach for his waist just as he pulls away, his hands still on my face. I'm almost in a stupor, furious he stole his lips away so soon. I manage to pull my eyes open, and I find that he's staring back at me, unblinking. "And I took you to a fucking bowling alley," he jokes.

We both laugh. Then, he takes my hand and leads me deeper into the room.

Even though we're the only ones here, we keep our voices low in reverence. He asks so many questions about the artists and how they created their pieces. I tell him what little I know—the exhibit is for an MFA studio on light and surrealism—and we read the various plaques, taking our time.

As we work our way through the exhibition, his hand strays to my lower back, then up to my shoulder blades underneath my hair. When we stand inside a swirl of candle-shaped bulbs that rotate slowly around us, he moves behind me and wraps his arms around my waist. He rests his chin on my shoulder, and I can feel the heat of him all across the skin of my back. His heart seems to beat in time with mine—or maybe that's just my heart beating doubly hard, more open and raw than it has been in years.

At the far end of the exhibit, James leads us into a little room that's sectioned off from the rest of the space. Somehow, I missed this before. It's a round, black tent with projectors hidden in three corners; dark pillows cover the floor, and at least a hundred mirrors hang all over the fabric walls, reflecting starlight in every direction. James lies down and raises an arm for me to lie next to him. As we stretch out, looking up at all the mirrors, it feels like we're floating through space. It's such a beautiful, all-encompassing sensation that I find myself wiping away a tear before I even realize I'm crying.

James lifts himself up onto an elbow and looks down at me. He runs a thumb slowly over my cheek. "I've never met anyone like you."

A pulse of excitement courses through my body, and I have to break eye contact, fixing my gaze on his chin. "I'm not normally like this. There's just something about tonight."

A grin comes to his lips. "I know what you mean."

He gently tilts my face up, and our eyes lock again. I can't help myself—I wrap a hand behind his neck and bring his lips to mine.

JAMES

As we kiss, Lucy pulls at the hem of my shirt, urging it off me, and I'm quick to tug it over my head. Her hands press on my chest, and she throws a leg over my hip. I sink a hand into her thigh, moving it steadily up under her dress. She pulls her body back just enough to make space for me to bring my hand to her stomach.

"Wait." I slide my palm back to her hip and extricate my lips from hers. It's the last thing I want to do, but this is escalating so fast. I need to make sure we're on the same page.

"What is it?" Her tone is impatient, but her eyes soften when they reach mine. She's clearly as caught up in this moment as I am.

"I just think we should take a breath."

"For what?"

I didn't expect her to question that, but I love how brazen she is. "Well, two things. First, how sure are we that there aren't security cameras in here?"

Lucy chuckles. "Sure enough."

She immediately begins kissing me again, and I talk against her mouth. "So . . . like eighty percent?"

"If that's good enough for you," she teases. I pull my lips away, and she gives me a sexy little pout. It's hard to resist.

"Second." I gently squeeze her hip. "Should we talk about where this is going?"

Lucy raises an eyebrow. "I'm pretty sure we already covered that. In detail."

"I mean for the rest of the summer. Or is this just tonight?" I can tell she has a witty comeback armed and ready, so I cut in: "Because I'd like to keep hanging out. Obviously it would be casual, no expectations. But I want to see more of you."

Lucy holds back a grin, but she seems undecided. "Oh, yeah?"

I muster all the confidence I have. "I like you. I don't want just tonight." I angle my face into her neck and kiss down her throat. "But if tonight is all I can have, I'll take everything I can get."

My lips travel lower, grazing the top of her left breast, and now Lucy is the one to pull away. "Then I have a question for you." Her eyes gleam. "Do you have a condom?"

LUCY

As our lips find each other again, my mind fixates on his hand on my hip, that hand that won't stop teasing me. I slide my body back again, urging his fingers between my legs. But he doesn't give me what I want, and the smile I feel against my mouth tells me he knows exactly what he's doing. Instead, he brings his hand under my dress, running his fingertips over my bra, delicately touching my breasts just above the line of the cups. Then he draws his fingers around to my back and, in one deft move, unhooks the strap.

He whisks me on top of him, sitting us both upright

in the same motion. It makes my heart race. His hands cradle the sides of my neck as his tongue moves against mine. Then his fingertips slide down my shoulders, take hold of my dress, and slowly pull it and my unclasped bra down to my ribcage.

I nearly gasp at the thrill of being exposed by him. My nipples were already hard, but when his lips drag across my breast while he traces his fingertips over my other nipple, my whole body shakes. He hasn't even touched between my legs, but the pleasure courses through me. When I don't think I can stand the tease any longer, I arch toward him. He responds by taking my whole nipple into his mouth and sinking his teeth ever so slightly into my flesh. This time, I can't hold in my gasp.

He pauses and makes direct eye contact, and I nod, breathless. His lips return to my nipple, and one hand cups my breast while his other hand finds my clit under the thin fabric of my underwear. I writhe against his fingertips and begin to climax almost immediately, grabbing him by the wrist to demand more, more. I see stars—though my eyes are shut tight—and I don't let him stop until I'm completely spent. Then I release his hand from my grasp—and the involuntary squeeze of my thighs—and collapse forward onto his shoulder, panting.

"Well," James says, a little breathless himself. "That was easy."

We both laugh. I feel lightheaded and the most at ease I've been all night, fully aware that his fingers are still pressed firmly against me, like if he let go, I might tumble over. "I don't usually come that fast," I murmur into the curve of his neck. "But very little about this night has been usual."

James responds with a wry laugh. "We're just getting started."

JAMES

Lucy's hair cascades all around me as she finishes catching her breath. My jeans have become my enemy—far too restrictive—and I'm eager to be rid of them. "So," she whispers from my shoulder, "where's that condom?"

She slinks off me, sliding her dress down her legs before settling back onto the cushions. Seeing her in nothing but her cotton underwear laid out on those pillows—there's something so free about it. About her. It's an image I want to hold on to.

I grab the condom from my wallet, pulling my jeans and boxers off and throwing them aside. Lucy strokes my shoulder, tracing lines across bone and muscle, as I roll the condom into place. I feel her eyes on me, scanning my face and body with anticipation. "Touch me again," she demands.

LUCY

James turns his body to mine and kisses me hard, and I can feel the full length of him on my thigh. Without taking his lips from mine, he pulls my underwear down, and I kick them away. I wrap a hand around him and slowly stroke, satisfied when he responds with a deep, low moan that sounds like it's been waiting to be unleashed all night.

He moves his hand between us, pressing firmly on my clit with his thumb, and slips two fingers inside of me. We both take a sharp breath as he curls his fingers up to my G-spot. The hum in my body is immediate, and I completely forget the concept of reciprocity. My executive function is gone as my fingertips dig into his shoulders, clinging tight. I can't even kiss him anymore. I throw my head back, writhing and whimpering under his touch.

When I can't take it any longer, I slap gently at his hand, and he drags his fingers up my stomach and breasts as I struggle once again to catch my breath. I feel his fingertips and eyes all over me, taking me in.

"Tell me when you're ready." His voice is a warm, low growl. When my eyes open to meet his, I'm still not completely recovered. My body is sated but continues to pulse with waves of excitement. "Because I'm dying to fuck you."

At those words, my skin is fully aflame again.

"Fuck me," I command, and the corners of his mouth turn up as he climbs onto his knees, pulling my legs wide around his. I watch his face, biting my lower lip as I wait for him to slide inside of me.

But he doesn't, not yet. Instead, he brings his thumb to my pulsing clit, and I feel it from my clenched toes to my outstretched fingers. With no headboard to grab on to, I grip the edge of the pillow under my head, squirming so much that he holds my body stable by pressing his free hand between my breasts. He looks to me to make sure I'm still with him, that this is what I want, and I manage a firm nod.

Then he plunges into me, and the sensation forces my eyes closed, my focus fully within. He thrusts, slow and deep, and I catch flashes of flexed pecs, the sheen of perspiration building at his collarbone and hairline. I dig my fingernails into his flesh, feel the heat of him all around me. He brings his thumb to his mouth and wets it, returns to circle my clit, and rocks into me deeper. The pleasure and the pressure are so intense that my whole body arches into him and my eyes burst open. It may be the most powerful orgasm of my life. I fix my gaze on his knotted brow as he lets out a hoarse grunt and falls forward onto me.

For several minutes, neither of us moves. Neither of us talks. We simply lie still, sweat slicked in each other's grasp, finding our way back to reality.

I let out a laugh.

He lifts his head from my chest and meets my eye with a quirked eyebrow. "What?"

"Just . . . after that, I *definitely* want to see you again."

James drops his forehead onto my chest, and I can feel his chuckle reverberate through my body.

VI

LUCY

The morning after graduation, I'm still asleep when my phone buzzes. I peel my eyes open to see James's name and adorable contact photo—which appears to be one of those oddly impressive doodles Rebecca mentioned, a scruffy dog chasing its own tail. My mind flashes to bowling victory dances, frayed menus, the starry tent. Did all that really happen in one night?

And I got my law degree.

My brain fails to compute the totality of it, to make sense of the fact that he's already texting me—just like he said he would when he dropped me off at the door of my building with a kiss goodnight.

I'm in a sort of stupor, staring at my phone, unable to act.

I've had some pretty good sex. Or at least I *thought* it was good. Nothing compared to last night. He never stopped paying attention to me. It wasn't like, "Oh, you had your orgasm? Cool, my turn." It never stopped being my turn. He read me like a book, sensed exactly what I wanted, and didn't always give it to me right away. He somehow knew I liked that.

So why am I finding the fact that he's texting me overwhelming?

I finally pick up my phone. He wrote, "good morning," and in a second message, "what are you up to today?" All lowercase, but full sentences, proper spelling. This guy knows his audience.

Now that my brain is partially online, I write back, "Still waking up, then buying ingredients for more French dip. Text you later?" He hearts the message. Good. Hopefully that buys me a few hours while I figure out what the hell I want to do.

I know what I *need* to do: get my damn grant proposal in. I already feel the stress that I set aside yesterday wriggling back into my veins. I have ten more days to finish it—alongside working my TA job and studying for the bar exam—so I'm going to need every available hour. Because if I don't get this grant . . . I don't even want to think about it. Keeping myself afloat in The Hague will be impossible without this money.

As I stare at the ceiling, failing to muster the energy to climb out of bed, my mind drifts to the backup plan I never allow myself to seriously consider. The job I applied for at the firm where I interned last summer. It's one of the biggest places practicing international law in the U.S. I interned at their Chicago office for a much-needed change of scene, but they also have offices here in New York and—it hits me—Portland.

On instinct, I roll to my side, open Google Maps, and type in "Newport." James's hometown. A two-hour-and-twenty-two-minute drive. If I were offered a junior associate position and chose that office, I could—

Nope. Lucy. Don't you even dare.

I sit up on my bed and splay my toes on the cold wood floor—the shock helps bring me back to my senses. I am *not* changing my plans for a guy. It's nice to have that job as a backup—they'll almost certainly make me an offer, interns always get offers—but the Portland office wasn't even on my radar before this morning.

My eyes wander to a photo pinned above my desk of my mom and me on a plane. Our cheeks squished together, big smiles on our virtually identical faces. We had gotten a rare upgrade to business class, and she acted like we had won the lottery, insisting that we commemorate our moment. I can't remember where we were going. It doesn't matter. It only ever mattered that we were together.

If I could tell her about James, she'd joke that I should definitely pick Oregon. "Get some!" she'd tease, and I would bury my face in her warm, soft stomach. She'd run her fingers through my hair as she laughed at her own bawdiness, scraping her perfect, almond-shaped nails across my scalp.

What she would *do*, though, is take the job that was best for her. For my entire life, she never put a man over me or her work. I know she dated, but she never even brought a guy home. Not once. Her priority was always her career. She seized every opportunity. And she shared every adventure with me.

I push myself off the bed and directly into my desk chair. I need to force myself out of my head. I open my laptop, and the window for the short list of International Court of Justice cases I want to weave into my proposal is waiting for me. I turn on a white noise track and get to work.

A few hours later, I meet Rebecca in the dining hall for lunch. My TA gig gets me extended student housing *and* a meal pass. Considering the budget I'm on, it's pretty clutch, and though carrying a tray amid a sea of undergrads can feel disorienting at this point in my life, there's also something comforting about overhearing tales of fake IDs and midterms. Rebecca starts at a top firm in Manhattan doing criminal defense in a few months, but despite her signing bonus, she's still game to be my date for bottomless cereal any day.

"Dude. What happened last night?" she asks, her eyes bright.

"It was fun." I shrug as nonchalantly as I can, which isn't very. "He took me bowling and we had dinner. How was the restaurant?"

Rebecca peers into my skull and stays there until I relent. "All right! Jesus." I feel a slight heat come to my cheeks as I whisper, "We hooked up, OK?"

Rebecca leans back, absolutely delighted. "You sluts! How was it? I mean, don't tell me any details, because ew, but was it good? Do you *like* him?"

I take a bite of my Rice Krispies, hoping the crackle will drown out any notes of uncertainty in my voice. "It was *very* good. He's awesome. And we're both leaving town in six weeks, so."

Rebecca waits, eyes still boring into me. "So what?"

"So . . ." I shrug again, and Rebecca scowls at me.

"You're not going to see him again?!"

"I don't know, maybe. We were very up front that it can't go anywhere—"

"To hell with that," Rebecca chides. "You two were so cute together! It was, what, like *three* minutes we all spent together, and I was already picturing your future babies."

I shake my head. "Dude, you've got to get a grip. We're about to move to opposite sides of the planet."

"So? Phone sex!" She points a stern finger at me. "*Face-Time* sex."

"Gross."

It goes on like that for a while, with Rebecca pushing hard for me to take James more seriously and me batting her back. Ultimately, we come to a compromise: I promise to text him after I finish my grant proposal.

I leave out the fact that I probably won't turn it in until right before the deadline. She'll be annoyed when she puts that together, but I've bought myself a week and a half, if James even remembers me by then.

JAMES

As I wait for my train home from work, I open my text conversation with Lucy—like there's any chance I could have missed a message. I'm trying to be chill, but it's been two full days, and she hasn't texted back. I know I told her I'd be OK if we just had that night, but now I'm feeling jumpy, like I'm going through withdrawal. I burned two dishes and broke a plate at work today. My friend—now my boss—was cool about it, but I need to get my shit together.

Maybe I just have to let Lucy go. My desire to live a small life in the small town where I grew up is an obvious red flag for her. I mean, she wants to go fight for civil liberties around the world. I want to make really good pasta from scratch. Where's the overlap?

And what I didn't tell Lucy is that I don't just dislike traveling. I kind of *hate* it.

It's stressful, and any time change messes me up for days, even if it's only an hour or two. Everything is always too expensive, too difficult to get to, too crowded. When a few friends in Philly invited me to join them on a trip to Peru, the whole thing was a disaster. I saved and planned for months, but when we got there, one of the guys wanted to just chill while the other wanted to hit every cultural site within a hundred miles, and I got stuck in the middle trying to make everyone happy. Sure, the ceviche was amazing, but the rest? No thanks. I prefer getting to know things well: walking the same strip of beach until I feel like I know every rock, testing a potpie recipe until it tastes like home.

Rubbing my temples with one hand, I reluctantly glance at the arrival countdown sign. It feels like my train has been five minutes away for the last ten minutes. I think about calling Rebecca to see if she has any inside info, but that feels over the line. Maybe I should send Lucy a text to say . . . what? I hope your day was good? Lame. And she could easily just ignore it, then what?

Then you should take the hint, genius.

I'm getting in my own head. I look back to my phone and type, "want to grab dinner tonight?" Delete, delete, delete. My second attempt: "have dinner with me"—no period. A period feels too pushy. I send it as my train arrives, but I make the absurd choice to wait for the next one in case she responds quickly.

LUCY

I've just managed to stop thinking hourly about James's hands all over my body when a text from him pops up on my laptop. "have dinner with me"—no period.

I'm at a good stopping point for the day. I finished grading all the quizzes from the class I'm TA-ing, got in a few hours of bar exam prep, and finished an extremely rough draft of the personal essay portion of my grant proposal. Plus, an annoyingly chatty study group has taken root at a nearby table in the law library. There's nothing standing in the way of me saying yes.

But as much as I want to see him again, I feel my chest tighten. I like him too much. Seeing him again feels like walking straight toward a hurricane.

Maybe I'm overthinking this? There's no way he's *actually* as kind and sweet and playful and fucking sexy as I thought he was the night we met. I was in a crazy emotional state. I was seeing the world through tear-stained, lust-tinted glasses. He can't possibly hold up.

And what if no-strings sex is just what I need to relieve the stress of this summer?

After several minutes of indecision, I text him. "Sorry, can't do dinner tonight. But I should be free around 11?"

Three little dots appear almost immediately. And then go away. And then they're back. I catch myself actually holding my breath, my shoulder muscles tensing, as I wait for his reply.

"11 tonight?" he writes. "that works. your place?"

I feel my cheeks burn. I'm already nervous—and excited.

VII

JAMES

I text Lucy from a bodega at 10:45, asking if I should bring anything. She responds quickly, "No need. I've got a bottle of red wine, if that's good by you." What I don't tell her is that the bodega is five minutes from her building, so rather than show up early like a real weirdo, I linger in the store—like a real weirdo. I keep tugging at my Dolly Parton T-shirt. I'm worried I might sweat through it before I even get there.

I have intense butterflies as I walk the last few blocks to Lucy's place. Clearly, she intends for this to be a hookup, and that's fine. But I don't know. Even though we've already had sex, it feels like there's now this pressure to perform? To be worthy of the call? To prove that it wasn't a one-off?

Fuck, am I nervous.

The last time I saw her was under her building's awning. I gave her a long, slow kiss, running a thumb over her cheek as she gripped my sides under my shirt. "Goodnight" was all I said as I walked away. It felt smooth at the time, but now I'm second-guessing everything. Maybe I should have asked to come up. Not let that magic night ever end. The crazy confidence I felt then is nowhere to be found as a soft *buzz* lets me inside.

She opens her door in an oversize black tee, no bra, and gym shorts, her caramel hair pulled back in a messy bun. I'm not sure whether to be encouraged or deterred by how casual she looks—is she showing me she's comfortable with me or reminding me just how low-key this encounter is meant to be? I can't focus with her nipples pressing into the threadbare fabric of her shirt.

We both stand at the threshold. I know my ears are red, but I see that her cheeks are a bit rosy too. "Hi," I manage.

"Hi," she responds. She closes the gap between us and gives me a hug. It feels friendly, not romantic, but at least she broke the ice.

She steps aside and ushers me past a bathroom door and cramped kitchen into her combined bedroom and living space. The studio is small but tidy—not much more than a bed, a sofa, a desk, some sort of rolling storage case, and a bookshelf overflowing with intimidating legal tomes. But the walls are almost completely covered by travel posters. Some are kitschy and pun laden, others have a retro vibe, and almost all have tattered edges.

Lucy picks up her glass of wine and pours a second one for me as I nod at a poster that declares, "Milan stole a pizza my heart."

"Are these all places you've been?"

She nods and hands me the glass, and we clink, failing

to meet each other's eyes. "I get at least one in every country. Some of them are really falling apart, but I don't want to frame them since I move around so much."

"Makes sense."

We stand in the center of the room as we sip our wine—which I can barely taste through my nerves—unsure what to do next. "I like your shirt," she says. "I have a similar one."

"Of Dolly?"

Her black eyes shine. "No, Miss Piggy." I scrunch my brow. "I guess I put them in the same category in my head," she explains. "They're both such badasses. Both bleached blonds."

I chuckle, feeling a little more at ease. "Who do you think would win in a fight?"

Lucy mock frowns at me. "They would never fight. I can imagine them running off together, though."

"I like that for them."

She steps over to the bed and sits down, and I use the opportunity to take a few gulps of my wine, hoping she can't tell how nervous I am.

"So," she says. "What should we do?"

I set my wine down on her desk, then sit on the bed next to her.

She turns my direction, tucking one leg in and casually throwing the other across my lap. My hand goes to her shin on instinct. There's no resisting running my fingers from her ankle to her knee and back again. Her voice is low, like it was in the art gallery, as she grips the collar of my shirt. "Take this off."

LUCY

Afterward, James and I are naked on my bed, both catching our breath. We finished on our sides, him lying behind me, an arm wrapped around my breasts.

I suddenly feel very exposed in the dim lamp light. Is there a way to wriggle away from him without being weird? His breath on the back of my neck felt sexy a moment ago, but now it feels stressful.

The sex was good. Very good. I climaxed twice, but I never fully let myself *go*. In the back of my mind, I never quite forgot that we would eventually come to this moment, the After Time, when I would still be very unsure what I want our temporary arrangement to be.

With James behind me, I'm grateful he can't see the uncertain look on my face, but I also wish I could sneak a glance at him. Does he have any idea what I'm thinking? Is he thinking the same thing? Or is he just in a post-orgasm haze, maybe drifting off, completely unbothered about what comes next?

JAMES

I feel Lucy stiffen ever so slightly in my arms. I'm not quite sure what to do or say, so I lift my arm off her chest into a stretch, and she responds by sitting up and fishing her T-shirt off the floor.

"Everything OK?" I ask, trying to sound relaxed.

She turns to me with a sweet smile, but a new one. Something about it feels slightly forced. "Of course."

As she grabs a fresh pair of underwear from her dresser, I hurry to take off the condom and drop it in her trash can. Then I slip my boxers back on. Once she's covered up, she picks up her glass of wine and takes a sip.

"Are you sure?" I scan the floor for my shirt but don't immediately spot it. "I didn't hurt you or anything . . . ?"

Her eyes dart to mine, and her face softens. "No. Not at all."

I sit on the edge of her bed, feeling lost, and I see her toes drum across the floor, like she's thinking with her whole body. "It's nothing like that, I promise," she says. She picks up my wine and hands it to me before sitting back down on the bed, positioning herself so she's leaned against her headboard, her knees by her chest and her toes grazing my thigh. "I'm just not very good at . . . this."

She says it with a slight blush, and it makes my whole body relax. I didn't realize how many of my muscles I was clenching. "Ah," I respond. "Same."

"Yeah?"

"I'm not exactly the show-up-at-a-girl's-door-at-eleven type."

She tucks her hair behind her ears. "The night we met was . . . I wasn't really myself. And I didn't know—" A strand falls into her face, and she blows at it. "I just don't want to give you the wrong impression. I mean, we talked about this, but I want to be *really clear*—"

It's like she's holding out an arm, keeping me at an

emotional distance, and I hurry to assuage her fears. "This isn't going anywhere. I know." I say it with a nod, like that seals it. She eyes me with a playfully raised eyebrow. "You're leaving, I'm leaving," I feel the need to add. "We don't want anything messy."

"Right."

I take a gulp of my wine for courage. "So what are you thinking? Just sex?"

She lets her head fall back against the wall, perhaps impressed that I'm willing to discuss this head-on. "Maybe. When do you leave, exactly?"

"My job ends July 31st, and then I fly to Oregon the next Monday. I think it's August 4th?"

She nods. "My flight is that Sunday. The 3rd."

Today is June 24th. I resist the urge to immediately calculate the number of days we have remaining.

"The thing is," she says, "I'm going to be really busy between now and then."

I don't love the immediate hedging, but I try to keep my tone encouraging, easygoing. "Me too."

"I really don't want there to be expectations." Her brow scrunches a little. "So maybe it *would* be best if we just . . . called it."

A fist tightens around my heart. It's stupid how much I don't want this to end. Not yet.

Somehow, I manage to push a grin onto my lips. "Are you breaking up with me?" She laughs, and I feel the grip loosen. Maybe I can still salvage this. "If you don't want to see me anymore, I get it."

She bites her lower lip. "It's not that. I do like you."

"I like you too," I tell her, my eyes locked on hers. "I really don't know much about you, but everything I know so far, I like." She holds back her smile, but I can see it in her eyes. "Honestly, if we get to know each other more, you'll probably be tired of me in a week. Or maybe I'll find out *you're* awful."

She laughs, and it's like fuel.

"That's what's most likely, right? So while we still like each other, maybe we should have some fun."

She watches me for a second, weighing her options. Then she presses her toes into my leg. "What kind of fun did you have in mind?"

A rush of desire takes hold. There are no nerves this time—at least not as many. I bring my hands to her hips, slipping my thumbs under the sides of her underwear as I pull her body down the bed. I slowly lift her shirt as I kiss my way up her torso, speaking into her skin. "Oh, you know. We could play a board game. Read . . ."

She chuckles as she pulls her shirt over her head. I give her a firm kiss, tasting the wine on her tongue, then work my way back down her body. Her hands instinctively reach for the headboard behind her as I pull her underwear all the way off.

VIII

LUCY

As we lie sprawled out on my sheets, James points out which of my travel posters are his favorites—South Africa, Morocco, and Germany. I tell him my goal of visiting at least ten countries in Asia, my least-explored continent, over the next ten years.

He draws a ballpoint pen tattoo on my arm of a pelican—my favorite bird—in flight. It's gorgeous. In return, I draw one on his chest of two stick figures fucking. He gives the stick figures names and backstories, then describes their torrid affair in detail. It makes me laugh until my sides ache.

By the time I notice the clock, it's after four, and we finally decide to crawl under the covers, still fully naked. I hadn't intended for him to sleep over, but now I don't want him to leave.

When I open my eyes the next morning, I'm face to face with that decision. James and I are smushed together, his hand splayed across my ribs. He's still asleep, and his mouth hangs open, a slight snore coming from the back of his throat. He's so fucking cute. I can finally take time to analyze that adorable freckle under his eye—really unlock its secrets—just as soon as I know how long I have before my TA gig.

As I reach for my phone, he cracks one eye open at me, then closes it again, wrapping his arm around me tighter. "I have to tell you something," he whispers.

My heart beats a little faster. "What?"

"You're naked under here."

I laugh, too loud for our proximity. "You are too."

He tilts his head down as if to check if that's right and then scrunches his face up, eyes still closed. "Shit."

I kiss the tip of his nose. How is he this charming first thing in the morning?

"What's your day like today?" he asks, slowly forcing his eyes open.

"My class starts at ten, then I've got to do laundry, bar prep, and work on my grant application."

"When is the bar exam?"

"Two months."

"And you're already studying?"

I try not to let the dark cloud of stress hovering over my head burst open and ruin this moment. "I started studying a month before graduation. I'm clocking about five hours a day."

James lets his eyes go wide, a playful terror in them. "Noted," he says, keeping his voice even.

He turns his head to yawn. "OK. Well, I've got an event this evening—an engagement party, I think—but I also need to do laundry. Want to do that this afternoon?"

At first I think he's joking, but he seems perfectly sincere. I give him a quizzical look. "You want to do laundry together?"

"Why not?" He smirks. "What could be more casual?"

A few minutes later, he's fully dressed, and I'm back in my tee from last night. We're standing at the door. "I'd kiss you," he says, "but I haven't brushed my teeth."

He shoots me one last sleepy, sexy look as he trudges down the hall, and I feel my insides twist. Despite myself, I hope that feeling lasts a few more weeks.

And then I hope he says or does something idiotic so I can move on.

JAMES

The next time I see Lucy, it's at a laundromat on Cornelia Street. We have a spirited debate about whether laundry needs separating: I put towels and sheets into their own load, and she throws everything in together like a monster.

The next night, she invites me to join her, Rebecca, and some law school friends at a roller-skating rink in Bushwick. She falls on her ass twice, laughing hysterically at her own clumsiness both times. She also somehow manages to make friends with the DJ, the woman renting us skates, and an entire bachelorette party. I can't keep the grin off my face.

Rebecca stares at us all night long with a big, creepy smile, and I have to pull her aside to tell her to chill. "I'm sorry!" she whines, not sounding sorry in the slightest. "I just want you two to get married and have babies that I'm a pseudo-aunt to!" I put a hand on her face and give her a playful shove, sending her gliding backward on her skates with a snicker.

The next night, Lucy and I watch *Hello, Dolly!* at her place, and I don't think she *loves* it, but she's clearly entertained. "I like how cynical it is," she muses over the credits.

"*Cynical?* It's got a whole song about falling in love in a moment!"

"Yeah, and it's got one about how having a wife is great because she'll do all the housework."

"Sure," I say with a head tilt, "but that's clearly tongue in cheek."

"And Dolly marries the guy for his money."

That earns Lucy a pillow to the face, which makes her cackle. "She does not," I counter. "She loves him!"

She hits me back, and I take it. "She *likes* him. But it's a beneficial arrangement, first and foremost, for both of them."

And then her mouth is on mine.

I want to pick our argument back up—to dig into her pessimism a little further—but I decide it's not worth the effort. All our conversations since the day we met have been surface level. Even the hours we spent talking after our second "date." We chat about our days, our likes and dislikes, but we haven't gotten anywhere close to the connection from that first night. I haven't heard her mention her mom since the diner, and when I try to ask her more about The Hague and her career, she switches the subject to what superpower I would choose or whether I've ever had a manicure. (I haven't, but I'm open to it.)

She also hasn't really asked me about my restaurant plans. Or my history. We haven't discussed past relationships, and there hasn't been any cause to bring up Miriam, my one serious ex. Miriam, who had my whole family tree memorized by our third date. She was so comfortable. Known. There's a level of comfort with Lucy too, but only when the conversation stays close to the surface. Whenever I try to dive deep, she slips away.

But I know Lucy isn't shallow or inconsiderate. She's just adamant about keeping this thing between us low-key, even as we spend all our limited free time together. It's tactical, and I'm sure it will make things easier for me too when we say goodbye in five weeks.

I've been trying to keep a mental list of things I don't like about her: She doesn't appreciate *Hello, Dolly!* enough, and she washes her sheets with the rest of her laundry.

Right now, that's it.

I'm pretty much fucked.

LUCY

I'm lying in bed, nowhere near sleep because this grant proposal is due *tomorrow*. It's after eleven, and I'm texting with James, who's on the subway heading back to his sublet after working a bat mitzvah. I send him jokes about how frazzled I am, but I'm *fully* freaking out. I'm convinced this proposal isn't good enough, but I've been staring at it so long I've lost all perspective on how to make it better, and I'm berating myself for not getting it done a day early so I could get Rebecca's opinion.

I'm tempted to call James and tell him this. Over the last week, I've been tempted to share all sorts of things. Like how the salty smell of his sweat after we have sex makes me feel strangely safe. Or how my mom, if she'd had the chance to meet him, would have gone on and on about how broad his shoulders are but then teased about his "undignified" blond hair. I want to tell him how I love the way he always walks on the street side when the sidewalk is narrow but also has no qualms about me holding a door for him. I want to tell him how scared I am that I'll be completely out of my depth at the UN International Court of Justice. And I want to hear about every girl he's ever dated so I can joke with him about his bad choices and secretly torture myself over whether I'm a better fit for him.

But instead I text a tired face emoji, followed by a winky face. I hate myself a little bit. The push and pull between wanting to lean on him and wanting to hold him at a safe, comfortable distance is getting exhausting. I just want to be myself and not have to worry. But there's so much to worry about.

He texts me back: "can I take a look?" I squint at the message for a moment, exhausted enough that I'm not sure what he means. "i'm no great writer," he adds, "but maybe some fresh eyes would help."

I frown and shake my head. He's just being kind. "No no," I text back. "The deadline's tomorrow, so there's no time." Then I add, "But thanks."

"it's not til noon," he responds, and I'm amazed he remembers the specifics. "plenty of time. send it now, if you're OK with me reading."

He's just off a ten-hour shift making fancy bar snacks for underappreciative rich teens. He must be exhausted. "No, really. That's very sweet, but you don't have to."

"i want to. send it already. we're losing time."

Still, I hesitate. It *would* be really helpful to get a second opinion. Even if just to boost my wilted ego. And if he gives terrible notes or tears the entire thing to shreds . . . well, it'll be a lot easier to break things off.

I open my computer and send him the Google Doc link to my seventeen-page proposal. I watch, unable to peel my eyes off the screen, as his little blue cursor appears next to my black one. I should close my laptop, maybe try to sleep for a few hours while he suggests whatever he's going to suggest. But I can't. His cursor sits at the top of the page, blinking menacingly. Then it moves into the third paragraph, and his first suggested edit appears. I wrote "compliment" when I meant "complement," and he's caught it.

That motherfucker. If he were here right now, I'd kiss him.

Forty-five minutes later, he's made it to the end of the document, and he's caught half a dozen typos. I text him how grateful I am for his edits, but he doesn't respond.

He's still in the document, now back at the top, adding comments. Most are questions, trying to understand my meaning in the trickier passages about specific legal cases. Some are suggestions for how to rework a sentence to make it more direct. By the time he reaches the end again, it's after two in the morning, my eyes are dry from watching him work, and he's made fifteen thoughtful suggestions. I won't take all of them, but I see the intention and care behind each note.

Then he calls me.

"You must be so tired," I answer before he can say anything.

"I'm wired from being around all those thirteen-year-olds," he says, a smile in his voice. "You're a great writer. The proposal is amazing."

I'm glad this isn't a video call, because my eyes well with tears. "Thank you. Really. Your notes are so helpful."

"Yeah? Good. It's easy to give notes on good writing." I can hear him pulling the phone away from his face to mask a yawn. "Now you should get some sleep, then give it one more look in the morning before you submit."

"Yes, sir."

"Oh, is it time for the sixth-date kink talk?"

I laugh. "Go to bed. And thank you again."

"You're welcome."

I fall asleep within seconds of my head touching the pillow, grinning like an idiot.

IX

JAMES

I set an alarm for noon, wake up, and immediately send Lucy a congratulatory text. Then I spend the rest of the afternoon cleaning my section of the apartment. I'm making her a celebratory dinner, and I've spent an insane amount of money on ingredients and too many hours on prep. This is her first time coming over to my apartment *and* my first time cooking for her. I want to get this right.

The place I'm staying is a cramped three-bedroom apartment in Harlem, and I share custody of the bathroom and kitchen with a dude from Russia who doesn't speak a word of English and a French couple, Chloe and Alba, who are here for four weeks producing a one-woman show about a mermaid with a fear of water. I haven't seen it yet, but I'm dying to. It sounds terrible.

Most of my stuff is sitting in storage pods in Philly, waiting to be shipped home to Oregon at the end of July—and I know Lucy knows that, but somehow, I still feel anxious about making a good impression. I wish I had the set of vintage whiskey snifters I found at a garage sale or the potholders my grandma quilted for me when I started to get into cooking. Anything that shows her a little more of me.

But I don't have those things, so I scrub the countertops, try not to think about the probably terrible notes I gave her last night, and put a solid extra hour of care into my menu: heirloom tomato salad with goat cheese, pork chops with a cherry pan sauce, and fresh-corn polenta.

When I open the door for Lucy, she has both arms up in the air and a bottle of prosecco in one hand, and she's glowing. "I fucking did it!" Her black linen dress rides high on her thighs.

"You fucking did it!" I hold out my arms, and she throws herself into them with no hesitation. When we let go, I'm surprised to see her wipe away a tear. "What is it?" I ask.

She's still beaming as she shakes her head. "Sorry." She laughs, seeming a little embarrassed. "It just occurred to me how proud my mom would be right now."

I grin and take the bottle of prosecco from her. "She would be. And I am. And you should be. So let's fucking *toast*."

I lead her into the cramped kitchen, where the air is heavy with butter and farmers-market produce. Lucy practically swoons as she walks in behind me. There isn't really a good place for her to sit while I finish cooking, so I pick her up and plop her on the counter next to the salad. She laughs and steals a tomato. "You know how to treat a girl right."

"I do what I can with what I've got. Drink?"

She nods, and I pop open the prosecco and pour it into tumblers—the best I can do. Lucy excitedly tells me about the relief and joy of getting her grant proposal in. She thanks me about eight times for my notes, which makes my ears go red. I still don't believe her that I actually helped, but I'll take it.

It really does feel like a weight is off her shoulders tonight. When she laughs, she throws her head back. She wiggles her dangling feet as she watches me work. She leans in conspiratorially like we're sharing a secret. It reminds me of the night we met. I feel like I'm getting a peek at the Lucy behind the wall once again. It's early, but I already want this night to go on forever.

But as I pull my pans off the stove, my phone buzzes. I check and see a new message from a bank. It's clear from the first words that it's bad news.

Lucy hops off the counter and puts a hand on my arm, immediately registering my disappointment. "What is it?" She sounds so worried it forces a smile onto my face, an attempt to reassure her.

"Sorry," I stammer. "It's nothing. We don't have to—"

"What is it?" She's adamant, seeing right through me.

"Just an email from a bank," I relent. "Another loan rejection."

"Another?"

I let out a sigh, failing to minimize the dejection in my voice. "This is the third in four days. No one likes that my grandma's house is my only real asset. I've got one more application out, but it's not looking good."

Lucy's expression is a mixture of sympathy and, perhaps, minor frustration. "I'm so sorry. Why didn't you tell me?"

I give her a knowing look, and her eyes drop to my chest. "Oh. Right."

I turn to my pork chops, carefully lifting them onto a platter. They look perfectly seared, and I want that to be enough. But I can't shake this disappointment. Should I tell her that five other banks told me I didn't even qualify to apply? That I've been looking for line cook positions in Oregon as a backup? That the market is so tight I might have to get some random day job to keep myself afloat? That my dream may have to wait for who knows how many years?

Would she really want to hear any of it?

The night feels suddenly spoiled, and I don't know how to fix it. We're commemorating a step toward her future, which we both know I won't be part of.

"Tell me about your grandma's house."

I turn to face Lucy, genuinely surprised. I raise an eyebrow, but she responds with a warm, tender smile, awaiting my answer.

I run a hand through my hair. It's such an innocent question, but for some reason it feels like she's just asked me to get naked. "Uhh . . ." I stumble and then feel the corner of my mouth curl up. "It's beautiful. Cedar shingles, right around the corner from the boardwalk. It's not huge, but it's got three bedrooms and a little balcony upstairs, and there's a big covered porch out front."

She's quiet for a moment. "Will you show me?"

LUCY

We sit at the table eating the insanely delicious food James has prepared. It's one of the best meals of my life, and I make an embarrassing number of involuntary sounds. "If you're trying to turn me on . . ." James teases.

I grin through a full mouth. "You're *sure* you don't have a Michelin star? How do we sign you up for that?" James lays a gentle hand over my whole face to shut me up, and it makes me laugh.

Between bites, he searches his phone for old pictures of his grandma's house. The Zillow listing is useless—just an exterior shot from probably twenty years ago. But as he sifts through family photos, he picks out the ones that best show off the built-in bookcases and oversize fireplace in the front room, the sunny kitchen with a formal dining room attached. He shows me a shot taken from the upstairs balcony of the sprawling ocean view—complete with a weathered lighthouse—and a few pictures of the downtown less than a block away.

In these same family photos, it's hard not to notice adorable little-boy James giving shy smiles to the camera, that same perfect freckle under his eye. When I zoom in on his grade-school face, present-day James reclaims the phone, trying to direct my attention back to the house, but I grab it back and zoom in on sweet shots of him playing cards with his grandma, getting a piggyback ride from his father, being read to by his mom.

Savoring the food he's made while looking through these

pictures makes them even more visceral, like I can smell and hear what it must have been like. Like I can picture this meal on his grandmother's table. "It's all so idyllic," I tell him, not meaning for my voice to come out as hazy as it does.

James nods, but hesitates before he responds. "It's weird—and kind of embarrassing—to now *own* this house and suddenly know how much it's worth. It's always been important to me, but that never translated into a monetary value in my mind, you know?"

"That makes sense." I look down at my plate. "But that monetary value isn't enough to borrow against?"

James shakes his head with a sad smile. "Not for an unproven cook with no other real savings." His eyes drop to a picture of his grandma sitting on the porch, working on the Sunday crossword and laughing at someone out of frame. "I could sell it . . ." He's smiling, but his eyes are somber as he meets my gaze. "I can't sell it."

I nod, wondering what it's like to be so connected to a place. I've never had that. I can't decide if it would be magical or suffocating. The idea of feeling pulled anywhere in particular strikes me as almost frightening. Home was always wherever my mom and I were. Now, it's wherever I am. But it's not the same. If anything, I find myself *more* compelled to regularly change up my scenery, my environment, my living space now that she's gone. Every new place to lay my head feels incomplete without her, so I keep searching for the next place that might feel better.

A vision of visiting James at his family home in Newport fills my mind. I wonder what it would be like to have his arms wrapped around me on that second-story balcony, looking out at a blue-gray sea that matches his eyes.

Then I remember something.

"Did you see that *New York Times* piece a while back about restaurants without traditional kitchens?" I ask. James furrows his brow and shakes his head. I feel my pulse quicken as I lean toward him. "It was about these great restaurants crammed into odd spaces around the city that only use hot plates and tabletop fryers and stuff. The big idea was taking an unconventional space and finding ways to make it work as a restaurant." James is still staring at me, not quite sure where I'm going. "What if you turned the *house* into your restaurant?"

I watch as James's gaze unfocuses and he leans back in his chair. I can't tell yet if he actually likes the idea, or if it's even feasible, but I'm already sold on it. Before I realize what I'm doing, I'm standing up and pacing in front of the table, rattling off the possibilities. "You could live on the second floor, keep that as your home. Then the downstairs and the porch become the restaurant. You don't even need hot plates! You already have a kitchen."

"A tiny kitchen."

"Sure, but you could start with that, couldn't you? And then maybe the dining room is storage or something?"

"Or a prep area," James almost whispers, his voice far off. I can see the wheels in his head turning, and it makes me even more excited.

"Sure! That!"

But then James's demeanor turns stony. His eyes fall to

the table. I'm at a complete loss as to what just happened. "Are—are you OK?" I stammer.

James forces a tight smile, and he seems almost embarrassed. "I'd have to rip out walls. Maybe turn the yard into a parking lot . . ." He shakes his head. "I don't know."

Right. This isn't just a house. It's his grandmother's house. His home.

My instinct is to go all-in. He'd have to change some things, but isn't it worth it? For me, it would be. But James and I are so different.

My shoulders sink. "I'm sorry. I didn't even think about that."

"No, don't be sorry." His features soften and he rubs the back of his neck. "It's a good idea. It's just . . . a lot."

I sit back down and resist the urge to say anything. I don't want to push him.

After a moment, I see the wheels in his head start to turn again. "I'd still need a big loan," he says, more to himself than me. "And zoning could be a huge issue." His eyes shift from side to side, as if he's walking through the house in his mind. "Maybe I *could* keep the structure mostly intact. Start small. A tasting menu and craft cocktails . . ." He tilts his head to the side. "Some updated fixtures wouldn't be the *worst* thing."

After a long, thoughtful moment, he asks quietly, "You really think I could pull it off?"

He sounds so uncertain. I pick up my fork and spend a good fifteen seconds cutting and assembling the perfect bite. Then I hold it up for James. He cocks an eyebrow at me but accepts it. I lean in close as he chews. “The man who made that . . . he can pull it off.”

James swallows with a tight-lipped grin. “Your confidence in me is terrifying.” Slowly, his shoulders soften, and I can tell the idea is still rolling around in his head. “It *could* work,” he says.

I hold back a grin, still wary of pushing too hard. “I mean, if you could have the house and your restaurant all in one . . . that could be pretty great. Right?”

He shifts forward and takes one of my hands in his. A corner of his mouth goes up, drawing my eye to his perfect freckle. “My grandma was very practical. She’d probably cuss me out if I *didn’t* try this.”

I lean over and kiss him a little more forcefully than I mean to. Before I realize what’s happening, he scoops me into his arms, his hands encircling my thighs. My legs wrap around his waist as he carries me through the apartment to his bedroom. “What about the leftovers?” I whine, only half joking.

“We’ll be quick,” he deadpans, and I laugh.

X

LUCY

Once we're both naked on his bed, I slide down his body to go down on him—it's never been my favorite activity, but the idea of being as generous with him as he's always been with me is a turn-on.

"Wait," he says, surprising me as I smooth my hands up his legs. Is it already obvious that I feel a little awkward?

But he just turns me onto my side, then tucks a few pillows gently under my head and shoulders so I'm propped up off the bed. He runs a hand up and down my body as he gets up on his knees near my face, positioning himself perfectly in front of my mouth. "This way I can see you better. And I can touch you too."

A thrill runs through my body. This is already so much better than what I had in mind. I take him in with my eyes and hand first as his palm glides over my hip. I lick him, then I look up, and he's grinning down at me. His fingertips slide between my legs and find my clit, and I have to lie back, already overcome. This no longer feels like something I'm doing just for him.

I feel eager, ravenous for him, and I take him into my mouth. His groans only amplify my full-body stimulation, and I let out my own moan when his fingers sink into me at the same moment that I pull him deeper into my throat. Within minutes, I climax with him inside my mouth.

I writhe in my ebbing waves of pleasure as he slides out from my lips and away from me. With my eyes squeezed shut, I'm barely conscious of him hurrying to get a condom on. I feel him climb on top of me, our bodies now aligned, and I claw at his chest, not yet sated. I open my eyes, still recovering as he looks down at me, waiting for my signal. I manage a little nod, then I feel all of him pound deep inside of me. I let out a gasp of ecstasy not suitable for a shared apartment, and he places a gentle hand over my mouth. I bite into the flesh of his palm, and we lock eyes as he rocks into me with all his weight. Then I squeeze my eyes shut again as he thrusts over and over, until he comes with a grunt.

He collapses onto me, his heart pounding wildly. I feel like I might faint. I see only him, and my mind is completely, perfectly blank.

JAMES

"The leftovers," Lucy whispers as I play with her hair. I don't want to get up, but she pushes me off the bed, and we sneak back into the kitchen in our underwear. I hold out a Tupperware, and she carefully packs up half the food. "I'm stealing this. Don't tell James," she explains to the container in a stage whisper.

When we make it back to my bed, we both sprawl on our stomachs, our noses turned toward each other, so close they almost touch. "What are you thinking about?" she asks. I feel caught, and she must see it. "The restaurant?" she guesses.

I nod. "*You're* still thinking about the leftovers."

She laughs. "True." After a long, quiet moment, her gaze shifts, as if she's trying to see inside my brain. "So a loan is still step one, I'm guessing?"

I love that she's so set on helping me figure this out, but I'm not fully sold on this idea. Making the whole bottom floor of my grandma's house essentially a public space. Remodeling. And what if the restaurant failed? I've always been someone who holds on to old things. This goes against all my instincts.

But I also meant what I said—my grandma would be *pissed* at me if I didn't at least explore this option. She would have loved Lucy's gumption.

"There are like four or five equally important step ones," I say. "Zoning, permits, licensing—but yeah, a loan is up there. If the house *can* become the restaurant, it would definitely be a much smaller ask. I could reapproach the same banks."

"Could you ask your parents for a loan?"

I give her a tight smile. "I mean, I think they could afford it. But they're kind of weird about money. I wouldn't want to ask."

"What do they do?" Her voice goes up like she's embarrassed not to know this already.

"They're elementary school teachers. Been at the same school together since they met."

"That's pretty romantic."

I let my shoulder roll backward, creating a little space between us. "It might have started that way, but they've had their share of tough years. When I was ten, my dad left for a week. But he came back. They always find their way back." I slide a finger under the strap of Lucy's bra, avoiding her gaze. "I love them, and I think they're happy. They like simple things, which I've always kind of admired about them. He gardens. She crafts." I hesitate. "I guess I've just always wondered what their lives could have been if they *had* let each other go." My mind jumps to Lucy's mom and her completely opposite sort of existence. "Teaching isn't as exciting as being a makeup artist."

"An internationally sought-after makeup artist." She raises a brow.

I put on a faux-serious look and a deep voice to match. "Of course. The very best."

"That's right."

"I'd love to see pictures of her work sometime," I say, and she responds with a soft smile.

"Have you thought about what you'll do? If you can't open your own place right away?" she asks.

I search her face. She's asking about my future. About my parents. Maybe her guard is just down temporarily, but it's intoxicating.

"I've thought about it, yeah." I shift my body forward so that our noses actually touch. "I think I'll still move back, try to find a job somewhere, though it might not be in a restaurant."

"No. You belong in a restaurant."

"It would be temporary."

She shakes her head, her nose rubbing against mine. "Unacceptable. You must make delicious, life-altering food. Always."

Thank god she likes my cooking. "Well, in that case . . . I don't know. It might make the most sense to turn the house into a rental for a few years, build up some savings. I could stay in New York and keep refining my skills before heading back."

"Stay here?" She seems startled.

"Yeah. Maybe. Why?"

Her cheeks flush, and she breaks eye contact with me. "Sorry. I just—" It takes her a moment to find her words, which is very unlike her. "When my clerkship is done, I'll probably come back here. To New York. I'd be traveling a lot for work, hopefully, but this will probably be my home base." She shifts like she's suddenly uncomfortable. "I haven't decided for sure," she hurries to add.

I feel like I've been punched in the gut. Multiple times. "Oh."

She's coming back here? The clerkship is only ten months. That's nothing. If I were to stay, we could—

"I might go to Chicago," Lucy interjects, as if she can hear my thoughts. "I'm not sure."

Right. *Get a grip, James.* You're fantasizing about a possible future with a woman who has no intentions of staying in one place, and none of the places she wants to be are in Oregon. Even if she did come back to New York, sticking around here would mean delaying my own dream. And to what end? There's no future where the lives we want intersect, not for more than a season.

I put on an easy smile. "This house idea could work. You might have cracked it."

She curls close to me and closes her eyes.

I think I love her is the last thought I have before I fall asleep.

XI

LUCY

As sunshine peeks through the window, I watch James sleep, and I imagine what he'll look like when he's forty, sixty, eighty. How his face will wrinkle, whether more perfect freckles will appear.

Then I realize I'm picturing myself as the aging woman at his side, creating visions of a shared lifetime.

What I'll wear to his third restaurant opening.

How he'll cheer inappropriately when I'm sworn in as a judge.

Where we'll fly the whole family for our fiftieth wedding anniversary.

I'm not *trying* to conjure any of these things, but it feels like my conscious mind has lost control and my subconscious is telling me what it has already decided. Like I have no choice in the matter. Like I might love him.

Fuck.

My heart feels like it might beat out of my chest, and I know I need to get out of here.

But looking at him, I don't want to leave.

Even as I'm freaking out, it is physically hard for me to pull myself out of bed and walk away from him.

What. The actual. Fuck.

I slip off the mattress as stealthily as I can and pull on my dress from last night.

This isn't *love*. It can't be. It's only been a few weeks. I have never fallen for someone like this.

I told a guy I dated in high school that I loved him, but I just thought he was hot. At sixteen, that felt like love.

I dated a guy all through our second year of law school, and I said *I love you* after four months, but I eventually got tired of him. I'm not sure now if I ever loved him or not.

But this. This feels different.

I've got to get out of here.

JAMES

I open my eyes, lift my head, and see that Lucy isn't there. On her pillow, she's left a note scribbled on a scrap of paper: "Need to get back for class. Stole some leftovers." I cradle my neck in my hands and close my elbows around my face.

Last night, Lucy fell asleep with her head on my chest, her hair cascading down my side. I don't remember having any specific thoughts as she lay there, just an overwhelming sense that everything was as it should be.

When I drifted off, I dreamt that Lucy and I were

walking cobblestone streets in some European city. I have no idea where—I've never been to Europe.

This is bad.

LUCY

On the way back to my place, I try to get a hold of myself. There are only four more weeks before I leave for The Hague, but I don't think I can risk this going any further. I need to cut it off. Cold turkey. Maybe even go on a date with someone else. That's always been my best remedy for getting over someone. Rip that bandage clean off and replace it with a fresh one.

I try to think of who from my class is still around. Or maybe one of my adjunct friends' friends? But my stomach turns, like it thinks I'm being disloyal to James.

The downtown express is delayed, and *fuck*, I want to go back to his place. I want to take a walk with him. I want to eat more of his food. I want to feel the weight of his body on top of mine.

I tap my foot like it's the commute that's making me agitated. I just need to think this through rationally. What are the benefits of seeing him more, what are the drawbacks?

If I keep seeing him, I could have a great last month in New York. But I risk falling for him even harder. The longing I feel right now, the heartbreak, could get much, *much* worse.

If I cut it off now, I'll still be thoroughly bummed, but it would give me time to work through all that and hopefully arrive in the Netherlands with a clear head, ready to focus on my career. Maybe even fall for someone planning to live a life like the one I want.

I can't imagine spending more than a long weekend in Newport. A sleepy little coastal town? Cute. For the rest of my life? No way. I need movement, adventure, new experiences. James wants routine and stability. That would drive me *crazy*.

My train finally arrives, and I feel more relaxed as I step on. Thinking this through is actually helping. It's not just that James and I are moving away from each other—even if we were in the same place, we wouldn't make sense together. We're built differently. I can see a look in his eye whenever I mention a far-off country I want to visit. It's a look that says, "I love that for you."

Maybe I don't actually love him at all. Maybe I'm confusing orgasms with feelings.

Still, I need to shut this thing down.

JAMES

I spend a solid twenty minutes in the kitchen staring down at my phone, trying to figure out what to do. I think I have to end this—the fact that it's no longer casual for me isn't fair to either of us.

My French roommates walk in and clock my distress.

Chloe pats my shoulder, while Alba hands me a bagel and murmurs, "Ce petit toutou." I don't know what that means, but I appreciate that they've basically adopted me as their little brother who probably outweighs both of them combined.

I could call to end things, but so much could go wrong. I could lose my nerve, or totally embarrass myself by "breaking up" with her when we were never really together.

I'll text her. Write something that makes it clear I need space. While maybe leaving the door cracked. Do I want that? The idea of shutting her out entirely is terrifying, even if I know in my head it's the smart thing to do.

I pick up my phone and write, "hey. thanks again for the house-restaurant idea. i'll probably be pretty busy digging into all that for a minute. enjoy the leftovers."

I read it three times, hit send, and wait, my heart in my throat. Five minutes later, Lucy responds. "Totally understand. I've got lots to do too." She ends her message with a pink heart.

OK. It's done.

I look up and realize a tiny French woman is leaning against each of my shoulders, reading the contents of my chat. "Eat ze bagel," Chloe says, patting my arm.

Alba nods grimly. "Carbs solve all ze troubles."

XII

LUCY

It's been three days since James texted, and I've felt every minute of it. That's how I know this is the right move.

Even though I know I was falling for him, I didn't expect detoxing to be this hard. I find myself wanting to reach out to him constantly, wishing I could share some tiny detail of my day. Like this morning: A student in the class I TA sneezed about twelve times in a row, the tiniest little sneezes I'd ever heard, and the entire class stopped and watched until it was finally over. Then the professor just carried on like nothing happened.

It was amazing. And it was also nothing. The kind of nothing you can only share with the one or two people who really know you, the people who understand your nothing moments.

I tell Rebecca about the sneezes over dark 'n' stormies at a dive bar on East Sixth Street where we used to have weekly "Judicial Oversight" happy hours with law school friends. That satisfies the urge for a moment. Then she asks what's going on with me and James.

"I don't know, it kind of fizzled."

"Bullshit," Rebecca proclaims.

"He told me three days ago he was going to be busy for a while and I haven't heard from him since, so what would you call it?"

Rebecca glares at me the way only a best friend can—scrutinizing and supportive at the same time. "Did you have a fight?"

"No." I sit up taller on my stool.

"You're sure?"

"Yeah, I'm sure. The last thing we talked about was his restaurant. I had this idea that maybe he could open it in his grandma's house."

After a long pause, Rebecca's glare softens ever so slightly. "Holy shit, that's brilliant."

"Thank you." I shrug. "I don't know if he'll go for it, though. He seemed attached to keeping every cross-stitched throw pillow in its perfect place." Rebecca raises an eyebrow at me, and it elicits instant and appropriate levels of shame. "Sorry."

"That woman *did* have a lot of cross-stitched pillows," Rebecca says. "Kind of like how someone I know has a buttload of travel posters."

My shame inches up another notch as I consider how hard it would be to let go of even one. "Point taken," I mutter.

I try to get the conversation back on track, sitting up straight again and taking a sip of my drink. "Anyway. It's not a big deal. He's probably just busy figuring out what he wants to do next, so . . . whatever." Rebecca's eyes narrow again.

"Please stop looking at me like that. You're giving me a headache."

"I just don't understand why you're being so blasé about this." She frowns. "You *clearly* like him. I've barely seen you since graduation, and I've tried to make plans with James like three times, but he's always been busy with you."

I shake my head, trying to seem perfectly chill. "Look, he's really nice, and we had a lot of fun." She sighs at my deeply boring description. "But we always knew there was an expiration date. It just came a little sooner than I hoped." I catch myself too late. "Expected."

Rebecca manages to keep a straight face, but I see the mischievous glint in her eye. She pulls out her phone and begins tapping. "What are you doing?" I ask, suddenly nervous.

"Texting James." I feel the hairs on my neck stand on end as Rebecca dictates, dramatically drawing out each word: "'What is going on with you and Lucy?' Send." She mercifully keeps her eyes on her phone as she waits for a response, and I pretend to be very interested in whatever baseball game is playing on the TV above the bar. What will James say?

Because I know why I want space, but why did he pull back? Is he really all that busy? We were both busy before, but we still found time to hang out. I almost feel like getting over my feelings for him would be easier if he sent a *hey, where'd you go?* text that I could then bravely ignore.

Rebecca's phone vibrates, and I catch myself shifting forward in my seat. She groans and tosses her phone on the bar as she recites his response: "what are you talking about?"

My brow furrows, unsure what to make of those words.

Rebecca downs her drink and flags the bartender for another. She either hasn't noticed the jumble of emotions in me or is giving me a pass. "Whatever," she grumbles. "If you two want to be withholding and weird, I don't know how to help you."

"We don't need help. But I do appreciate your concern."

She spins to face me as the bartender slides over a fresh cocktail, and her eyes are the softest they've been all night. "I'm sorry. I know I'm being pushy. I just love you, and I love him, and the thought of you two falling for each other was too perfect."

I give her a little smile. "Sorry to let you down."

"Yeah. You should be."

We share a grin and both sip our drinks. "If it helps, I really do think he's great. Maybe if things were different, this could have been something."

"You think so?"

Her tone has lost its edge now too, and for some reason, it makes me want to open up. Speaking in hypotheticals feels easier and less high stakes than discussing my real, current feelings. "I don't know. He's very sweet. I always felt safe with him. Like I could fully be myself. And we had a lot of fun. Like, *a lot*."

She crinkles her nose. "I don't need to hear the details."

I laugh. "He's . . . good. Definitely the kind of person

I'd want to end up with someday. Someday being, like, ten years from now."

"Sure," she says. "You can't take dating in your twenties too seriously."

"Exactly. This is when we experiment and try people on."

"For sure."

We've always been on the same page about this. But I never know when someone's internal switch is going to flip on love and marriage and babies. It's already starting to happen with a few of my slightly older law school classmates. One day a friend will be swearing off relationships forever and imagining buying a house with four friends, then suddenly she feels like she has to marry her crappy boyfriend because the clock is running out to have kids—which she didn't even want yesterday—and surely no one else will ever love her as much as the guy she happens to be with right now.

I shake my head at Rebecca. "As much as we clicked, honestly, James and I are very different. It sounds like he'd be happy to move back to Oregon and never leave. Like, *ever*."

Rebecca tilts her head like that might be right.

"And last I checked, there aren't too many international human rights cases going down in Newport."

"Very few," Rebecca deadpans.

I shrug, trying to comfort myself as much as Rebecca. "So there you go. Couldn't have worked regardless."

"I guess," Rebecca sighs. "But love is supposed to conquer all, right?"

I give her a half smile. "Good thing I don't love him."

JAMES

It's been a week since my last message to Lucy. I've wanted to text or call her about eight thousand times. When I ate the last of the leftovers. When a kid on the subway sang "Tomorrow" from *Annie* at the top of his lungs for no apparent reason. When I found one of her hair ties in my pocket. But so far, I've managed to resist the urge.

Because as much as I've been itching to reach out, I haven't heard a word from her. No check-in to see if this house-restaurant idea will work out. No little messages about something cute or random that happened. Nothing.

With each hour that passes, I feel more and more certain that I'll never see her again. At least not romantically. Maybe in a few years, we'll cross paths at Rebecca's wedding, and she'll be like, "Oh, yeah. Jason, right?"

To distract from my wallowing, I've been picking up extra catering jobs—sometimes doing two gigs a day—and making truly excellent food. Shredded pork bao. Soft pretzels from scratch. Mini lobster rolls.

On my one day off, I threw myself into getting answers about the restaurant. I talked to a city planner in Newport who said rezoning my grandma's house for commercial use would be an annoying process, but doable since it's so close to downtown. The same goes for licensing and permits—all long slogs, but possible. I started an updated proposal to get the capital I need, which is now about a quarter of my original ask, and I bought a little notebook so I can sketch out different floor plans, logo designs, and place settings on my commutes.

And the more I sit with this idea, really process it, the more excited I become. It still feels weird changing so much of a house that I have so many memories in, but the idea of giving it new life, new purpose, letting it be part of my dream—it just feels right. And I never would have considered it without Lucy.

It'll be months, maybe over a year, before I can actually open, but the sooner I get back to Oregon, the faster everything can go. I tell myself that leaving in three weeks is something to look forward to.

That's how I manage the days.

But the nights are another problem.

Tonight, I hit my bed, and I just want to sink into it and never get up again. Tonight, I wonder if she's already seeing some new guy who summers in Italy or works in finance.

Tonight, I wonder if Miriam and I will get back together.

She loves Oregon the way I do. She once said she couldn't imagine living anywhere else. I don't even know if she's still there, or if she's single, or if she'd want to hear from me. But lying in bed, I pick up my phone and toy with the idea of texting her to find out.

But what greets me is a note from Rebecca: "Bday party for ME on my roof next Sat. You're cooking. Get excited. Yes, Lucy's gonna be there. Don't be weird."

Well, fuck.

XIII

LUCY

Rebecca's invite says the party will start promptly at 5 p.m. and "go late." Awesome. She's having it on the roof of her Lower East Side building and has invited law school friends, soon-to-be coworkers, and everyone who lives on the top floor to ward off noise complaints. That includes Mrs. Jenkins and Mrs. Howard, two little old ladies whose husbands inexplicably died within a week of each other thirty years ago. Rebecca says Mrs. Jenkins and Mrs. Howard have been "roommates" ever since.

I resolve to arrive at 6:15, hoping Rebecca will already be tipsy and won't notice when I slip away in an hour. I can avoid James for an hour.

Not *avoid* avoid. I'll say hi. But I won't linger. Just a casual, "Oh, hey," and then I'll introduce him to my super-hot date while being *very* chill. The chillest. James will be amazed at how chill I am. And maybe a little jealous.

OK, get it together. I take a deep breath and exhale as slowly as I can.

Asher, my date, should help with that. He's getting

his master's in electrical engineering at NYU. My friend Zoe knows him—I can't remember how. What stood out from our conversation were words like "cute," "smart," and "I'll give him your number." That's all I really need for tonight's purposes: someone who can pass as a reasonable, nondesperate party companion.

Walking into the party, I spot a rented karaoke setup that Rebecca probably spent way too much money on and a makeshift dance floor. In lieu of seating, she's lined the perimeter with pool floaties in the shapes of sharks, unicorns, and swans.

And, naturally, there's a Slip 'N Slide. Rebecca seems to have set it up in such a way that the excess water runs toward a drainpipe and not through her neighbors' ceilings, but still. "Someone's going to break a bone," I quip.

"Yeah. Me," Asher jokes.

He really is beautiful. I've already wondered more than once why he would possibly need any help from Zoe getting dates.

Still, even in his presence, I can't stop myself from looking for James. It takes me seconds to spot him. He's ten feet from the food table, facing away from me, a beer in one hand, his arm wrapped around a beautiful girl.

JAMES

I arrived early to set up the food. With Rebecca's approval, I went with my versions of picnic classics: stone fruit skewers with lime zest, pigs in a blanket with andouille sausage, fried chicken on waffles with hot honey in the batter. I want Rebecca to be happy—partly because I love her, partly so I can escape this party as soon as possible.

I spot Lucy the moment she walks in. Honestly, I've had one eye on the door the entire time I've been here. Rebecca graciously warned me Lucy was bringing someone, but I am not being nearly as cool about it as I promised myself I would be.

Of *course*, she shows up with a goddamn Adonis. Probably from her law school. That place must be crawling with sinewy trust fund bros dying for the chance to take her out.

I shake my head, annoyed at myself for being so bitter. Lucy is free to do what she wants, same as me. She doesn't catch me staring, and I'm able to turn away and put on a good show of being nonchalant. Now, if I can just convince myself to actually *be* nonchalant, and maybe take some more interest in my own date.

Delia is a waitress at my catering company. She moved to New York six months ago from Chicago in the hopes of breaking into theater. I honestly don't know much about her beyond that, but we once spent half an hour at a wedding we worked coming up with outlandish reasons why the mother of the groom seemed so pissed at the priest. Maybe he was her estranged stepbrother who could only get an invite by posing as an officiant? Or maybe he borrowed money from her to start a dog grooming business and then refused to repay her when he changed course and became a man of God? We had a good laugh, and I got her number.

I met Lucy the next afternoon.

But yesterday, at a banquet, I felt someone nudge my shoulder. Delia whispered that she'd found out the truth: The mother of the groom was having an affair with the priest's hairdresser. I asked her out on the spot.

LUCY

I'm not in any rush to fake being casual in front of James, so I pull Asher in the direction of the drinks. Alcohol will help. I fish through the cooler for some sort of canned cocktail, but Asher redirects me to the cheap beer. "Gotta pace ourselves. How will we have the stamina to hog the karaoke machine all night if we're plastered?"

A little of the tension leaves my shoulders. "We really don't have to stay that long. I just needed to make an appearance—"

"Heresy!" It's Rebecca, dressed in a satin tube top with a matching floor-length satin skirt.

I laugh and grin, shaking my head lovingly at her. "Is that your prom dress!?"

"Fuck yeah it is! How many more birthdays will I have where this motherfucker still fits?"

Asher puts his hand up for a high five. "You look amazing."

"I like him already," Rebecca says, slapping his palm.

I introduce them, and she gives Asher an approving once-over before waving him away.

"I need to talk to Lucy. Go chat with Mrs. Jenkins and

Mrs. Howard. They're lesbians and murderers. You'll love them." A confused Asher follows Rebecca's pointed finger and obediently steps off to find what destiny awaits him with the octogenarians chortling in the corner.

Rebecca steps closer and lowers her voice as we watch Asher greet the delighted old ladies. "*He's* very cute."

"Right?"

"You know who else is cute? My cousin. The one you're pretending not to be into. James. James Marcus Shaw. Remember him?"

"Who?"

Rebecca pokes me in the ribs, making me laugh. "I gotta say, you both coming with random-ass dates feels very tryhard."

"James hasn't texted me in two weeks."

"Have you texted him?"

"Nope. So there you go."

Rebecca gives an exaggerated sigh, and I respond with a tight side hug. I *am* sorry she won't be getting this particular birthday wish, but talking about James when he's within a hundred feet of me makes me feel itchy.

We turn our attention back to Asher, who has Mrs. Jenkins and Mrs. Howard giggling like teenagers.

"Seriously, where'd you find this guy?" Rebecca asks. She's fully ogling him, and I should be too. But before I can stop myself, I look across the roof at James—and he's looking back at me. His expression is neutral, as if he's lost in thought. But as soon as our eyes catch, he stiffens.

And here we go.

JAMES

And here she comes. Guess it's time to get this over with. I press a casual smile onto my face, and I get the distinct feeling that Lucy's is just as forced. My arm is wrapped loosely around Delia's waist as she chats with one of Rebecca's college friends, and I give her a little squeeze, which makes her grin up at me. She's probably eight inches shorter than Lucy—the top of her head barely comes to my shoulder. I miss looking at Lucy at eye level.

And I miss the feel of her hair. The sound of her whisper. With every step closer, I'm in increasing danger of falling back into her gravity.

But no. She's coming over here just to be polite. It'll be over in a minute, and then I can give all my attention to the woman I brought to the party.

"Delia?" Lucy gasps, ten feet from us.

"Lucy!" Delia exclaims. "Is that you?"

Before I can register what's happening, Delia slips out of my grasp and runs over to Lucy, wrapping her in a bear hug.

"Oh my god, Delia! What are you doing here?" Lucy asks.

"I just moved to town. I'm an actor. At least, I'm trying to be."

"That's amazing! I'm so happy for you!" Lucy beams.

"Well, don't be too happy. So far I've booked an off-off-Broadway production of *Cats*. It's not even the musical. It's a one-act drama. About cats."

Now they're both laughing, and I feel like I've been hit in the face with a shovel. "Sorry, how do you two—?"

"Lucy and I were best friends from, like, eighth grade to eleventh? She was always traveling, but we'd write each other letters until she got back. Then my family moved and things got a little crazy—"

"Oh my god, how's your sister?" Lucy jumps in.

"*So* much better." Lucy and Delia slip right into old times, giving me an opportunity to put the pieces together, or try to. They know each other. That's . . . good? It's not *bad*? Except now they'll want to talk all night, which definitely ruins my escape plan.

LUCY

As I catch up with Delia, I'm simultaneously trying to sift through this unexpected twist of fate. James is dating Delia? Have they slept together? What does this mean? It shouldn't mean anything to me. But.

"I'm sorry," Delia says. "This is my date, James." His blue-gray eyes meet mine, and he seems just as bewildered as I am. We stare at each other stupidly for a few seconds before Delia catches on. "Do you two know each other?"

Oh, do we.

I hope that James will speak first and save me from having to explain whatever the hell our connection is, but he's just standing there, frozen.

Rebecca glides over to our little group. "Lucy is my

best friend, and James is my cousin," she tells Delia. I'm grateful for the save—but I also know she's relishing this whole situation. Rebecca doesn't know anything about my friendship with Delia, but she must have overheard enough, because she looks completely and annoyingly tickled.

"Got it." Delia smiles. "So you're all friends?" This time Rebecca doesn't respond. She keeps her mouth firmly shut and looks eagerly between James and me as we both . . . just stand there. Oh god. I can feel the heat rising in my cheeks, and I see the familiar red at the top of James's ears. If Delia didn't pick up on the weirdness before, she definitely has now.

"You were right, Rebecca." Asher startles all of us, appearing behind me and throwing an arm around my shoulders. "I'm in love with Mrs. Howard and Mrs. Jenkins. I want them to adopt me."

Rebecca laughs. I realize I've forgotten to breathe for the last ten seconds and take a deep inhale, reminding myself not to freak out. Maybe the worst is over. I can introduce Asher, grab Delia's number, and get the hell out of here.

Yeah, maybe this won't be terrible.

JAMES

This is terrible. Now that I know Delia and Lucy are old friends, any attraction toward Delia evaporates. Dating her suddenly feels wrong.

But maybe I can still figure out how to act normal. All I

have to do is shake the hand of this too-handsome bro without launching him off the roof, and everything will be fine.

"Delia, James, this is Asher." I notice the slight tremble in Lucy's voice as Asher holds out a hand, which Delia shakes kindly and I grip too firmly.

"How long have you two been together?" Delia asks.

"Oh." Lucy fidgets with her pale-yellow dress a little, but her voice doesn't shake this time. "This is actually our first date. We met through a mutual friend."

Asher gives Lucy a funny little look, and everyone clocks it. I watch Lucy's brow furrow. "Sorry. Should I not have said 'date'?" she stammers.

"No, no. That's fine. I just wouldn't describe Zoe as a friend."

I look between them. What is happening right now?

"Oh. How would you describe her?"

"She's one of my partners."

LUCY

Silence falls.

"Wha—what do you mean, 'partners'?" I ask, trying my best to keep the tone light.

Asher doesn't seem embarrassed in the slightest. "I mean romantically. Zoe and I are poly. I'm so sorry, I thought she told you."

My mind is spinning. Is it possible I'm so self-centered that when a person offers up their own boyfriend to date, I completely miss that massive detail? I glance at James and am grateful to see he has suddenly found the tops of his shoes very interesting. But Delia and Rebecca can't peel their eyes off Asher and me. "I, um . . . she and I must have miscommunicated," I mumble.

"So wait," Rebecca jumps in—like *now's* when I need her. "Your partner sets you up with other people?"

"Sure." Asher seems to have all the nonchalance I was striving for. "We're always looking out for each other, helping each other find like-minded people we can connect with."

Rebecca can't help herself. "How many partners do you have?"

"That's a pretty personal question." Asher doesn't seem offended, but he's setting a clear boundary, and Rebecca reluctantly backs off.

I feel like the ground has turned to jelly under my feet. Asher turns to me with a lowered voice. "Should we go talk? I guess I assumed since you're leaving soon—"

"Leaving? Where are you going?" Delia is genuinely disappointed, and I'm grateful to talk about literally any-fucking-thing else.

"Oh, The Hague. I leave in two weeks. Same as James."

JAMES

Now Delia turns to me. "Wait, what? You're moving to the Netherlands?"

"No!" I laugh nervously. "No, I'm moving home to

Newport. Oregon." Delia stares at me in disbelief, and my stomach drops. "I told you that. Didn't I?"

Delia's face turns to stone before my eyes. I watch as any attraction she felt for *me* evaporates. "No. You didn't."

The scene is so awkward at this point that even Rebecca can't enjoy it. "Who needs a drink?" she practically yells. Reflexively, everyone reaches for the nearest, hardest alcohol they can find.

"You know what this party needs?" Asher offers, offensively charming. "A really bad karaoke song. Lucy, you want to—?"

Lucy struggles to form any sort of response. But Delia squeezes her hand, then turns to Asher. "I'll sing with you. But fair warning, I'm really bad."

"Perfect."

Delia follows Asher to the karaoke machine with a warm smile at Lucy, and I catch Lucy mouthing the words *thank you* back.

Rebecca has made herself scarce, I suddenly realize, and Lucy and I are alone. Her eyes meet mine.

I have no idea what the hell to do, and it doesn't look like she does either.

"I didn't know you were poly," I mumble.

She stares at me long enough that I think she might just walk away without responding. Then she smirks. "Neither did I."

We both chuckle, and the tension breaks, at least for a moment. "I can't believe you and Delia know each other."

"She's actually really cool. She and you—"

"There is no she and I, not after this. Pretty sure that bridge has burned. From both ends."

Lucy represses a grin, and it feels like she's glad. I hope she is.

"How's it going with the restaurant?" she ventures. "Do you think you'll—"

"Oh yeah!" My voice is too loud, like I've forgotten how to talk. "There's still a lot to figure out, nothing's certain. But yeah, it's looking good. Permits, zoning . . ." I want to tell her every last detail, but I limit myself to "I think you solved it. Thank you."

Lucy's cheeks color faster than I've ever seen. "I hope you don't have to change the house too much."

"I don't think I will, actually. At least not at first." I lean a little closer to her. "I'm kind of looking forward to ripping out the paisley wallpaper."

As much as I was dreading this encounter, now I don't want it to end. I want to feel like we used to feel, to talk like we used to talk. But maybe she's just being polite, secretly itching to get away.

So I rest a hip against the edge of the roof, settling into this location and, I hope, signaling to her that she can either take a lean with me or graciously make her exit.

Immediately, she presses her lower back against the roof's edge alongside me, our bodies inches apart, both angled toward the party. The breeze blows her hair onto her cheek, and it takes all my self-control not to brush it behind her ear. But I have no such strength when it comes to stealing a glance at the hint of cleavage exposed by her dress.

LUCY

Leaning next to him was instinct. My body did it without my brain getting a say.

I feel drawn to him like a magnet. Now that we're perched next to each other, I feel almost drunk—though I've only had a beer and a half. All the rationalizing I've done over the last two weeks is out the window, and the only clear thought I can muster is, *He's looking at my breasts. Maybe I should unbutton my top button so he'll look even harder at my breasts. God, I wish it was his lips and not his eyes on my breasts . . .*

I sip my drink, very much stalling as I try to figure out what to say. Is there anything I *want* to say? I honestly don't know, but I know I don't want him to walk away. I'm pretty certain that as soon as one of us leaves this party, that will be it for us. And I'm not ready for that to happen.

"I will admit," he says, breaking our silence and tilting his head conspiratorially toward me, "I was nervous about seeing you. But I didn't expect it to go *that* badly." Now his eyes are on mine, and god, I've missed them.

My heart is racing, but I try not to show it. "You were nervous to see me?"

James turns his head back toward the party and gives an exaggerated shrug. "Nah." It's so clearly a lie that we both chuckle. "Were you nervous to see me?" he asks.

My stomach flips. Something in his tone tells me he hasn't forgotten what we're capable of when we find ourselves alone. My rational brain clicks online and yells,

Alert! Alert! Keep your guard up! But I don't want to listen. Instead, I mimic his nonchalant response. "Nah."

I'm pretending to survey the crowd, but I can feel his smile. I have the urge to lean my body against his, to feel his skin pressed to mine. I'm growing more and more certain he wants the same. For this moment, for the night, for as long as possible—I have no idea. And right now, I don't care.

But no. Fuck. This is *exactly* what I've been trying to avoid for the last two weeks. I hold my sweating drink to my chest, hoping the cold shock will slow me down. "I should really go," I say.

We're both looking forward, watching the party, but I can feel his body tense. In my periphery, I see him open his mouth then close it again. I'm dying to know what he's thinking. "No, you stay. I'll go," he says after a moment.

"You don't have to do that."

"I was planning to leave early anyway. And I'm guessing Delia won't exactly be eager to hang around."

So this is it. One of us will leave, and that will be that. I can feel the blood draining from my face. Then my eyes drift over to the karaoke setup. "I wouldn't be so sure of that."

James glances at me, and I nod in the direction I want him to look. Together, we watch Asher and Delia sing "Sex on Fire" by Kings of Leon. Terribly. Asher touches Delia's arm, and her hand lands on his chest as they stumble giddily through the bridge. The energy between them is undeniable.

Not even a hint of jealousy registers in my brain. "Good for her."

James nods. "She could do a lot worse." I turn to him, and he raises his eyebrows in an adorable way, clearly referring to himself.

I start to laugh, and once I do, I can't stop. It's like all the pent-up anxiety of seeing him has come to the surface and exploded out of me.

James laughs at my laughter, and soon, we're both overcome. It feels fucking great. We laugh so hard that I hunch forward, my hands on my thighs, and I feel his palm press into my shoulder blade as if to balance himself. I'm so glad I'm already looking away when it happens because my cheeks burn at even this friendly touch.

I let my arm come to rest against his as we both recover, and the last of my resolve evaporates.

"Fuck it," I say. "Let's stay."

James gives me a sideways smile, then he taps his beer can against mine.

As I wipe away tears, I spot Rebecca by the food table, watching us with a devilish grin.

XIV

JAMES

I feel like I'm levitating above my body as Lucy and I chug our drinks. Or at least Lucy tries to chug, then starts laughing again and spits. "I'm not very good at this." Her black eyes are at their brightest.

"You can't be great at everything," I tease, and she presses a hand into my chest. I reflexively cover it with my own, so eager for every touch I can soak up, every sensation I've pined for over the last two weeks. I want to pull her into my arms and kiss her right now, but I'm still not sure exactly where we stand. So instead, I take her fingers in mine. "Come on. We're dancing."

As we pass the karaoke setup, Asher and Delia are on to Lionel Richie's "All Night Long"—which is somehow even sexier than the last song—and they've graduated to holding hands as they serenade each other. Definitely better off without us.

No one else is on the floor yet, but when I spin Lucy, half a dozen other people hurry to join us, apparently glad someone broke the seal and started the party in earnest.

We dance near each other, not necessarily together, but whenever the chorus hits, we can't help pressing our bodies together, finding a matching sway in our hips, and belting out the lyrics.

I find it nearly impossible to keep my eyes off Lucy's face, her breasts, her hips, her hands. At one point, I forget to move at all as I watch her hips shake, dumbstruck. She catches me, grins, and throws her arms over my shoulders. I wrap mine around her waist and feel her relax into me.

"I've missed you," she says.

"I've missed you too."

We're still swaying, but not to the rhythm. "So why didn't you call?" she asks.

"Why didn't you?"

"You initiated this. You go first."

I'm too in the moment to think, to second-guess myself. "I was getting too attached."

I feel her hand grip the back of my neck. The smallest crease forms between her brow. "Really?"

I nod. "You're amazing, Lucy. I didn't know how to—"

Before I can explain further, her lips are on mine. I feel a rush of blood coursing through my body as I sink into the kiss, holding her so tightly that I lift her off the ground. I run my hands up her back, then down to her hips. I know she can feel my excitement. All I want is to be inside her.

She pulls her lips from mine. "Follow me," she whispers in my ear.

LUCY

I lead James behind the roof stairwell, where a wall shields us from the party. There are buildings surrounding us, but the sun has almost set. We're veiled in shadow.

I press my back against the wall and pull James to me. I feel him getting harder as his lips and tongue run from my neck down to my chest. "Do you have a condom?" I murmur, and he suddenly pulls his head back, a heartbroken look in his eyes.

"I don't, actually."

I don't know why that makes me so happy, that he didn't start this night planning to have sex. It also doesn't hurt to see him so devastated at the idea of not getting to fuck me. I fish into my purse. "I might."

"Oh no," he groans in an endearingly over-the-top way, his lips returning to my neck. "Were you going to have sex with that Greek god?"

I laugh, then finally find a condom tucked into the interior pocket. I triumphantly hold it up to show him, and we're both smiling as he kisses me. I push him back for a moment to pull my underwear off, and he turns to the side to undo his pants just enough to get the condom in place. As he brings his lips back to mine, I stuff my underwear into his back pocket. "Hold these for me?"

He grins and slides his palms under my dress, up my hips and thighs. "Anytime."

Then he lifts my right leg, pulling my whole body slightly up the wall—still warm from the day's sun. My hips reach out to him, practically begging him to enter me. He kisses me with urgency, but he makes me wait, the length of him pressed against me. It's like he wants to hold on to this moment, and so do I. My whole body is buzzing in anticipation.

Then he presses his forehead against mine and slowly, deeply glides into me. All the longing and anxiety of the last two weeks crumbles, and I feel an overpowering mix of relief and serenity. I groan, and he hooks his elbow under my knee to bring my raised leg higher. With his other arm, he braces against the wall so his head is next to mine. I bury my teeth in his shoulder to muffle my sounds of pleasure. His hot breath is on my neck: "God, I've missed fucking you."

As he starts to increase the intensity, each thrust has me thrumming toward climax. Orgasm overtakes me, and I press my foot into his calf, seeking some semblance of steady ground. If he let go of me now, my legs might give out entirely. When I'm at my absolute pleasure limit, I tell myself to hold on. I brace, and he comes with a long, guttural exhale.

We stand there, him inside of me, my leg still slung over his arm, catching our breath. After a long moment, he releases my leg and gently smooths my dress back into place. Still trying to catch my breath, I close my eyes and hope I won't accidentally slide down the wall onto my ass as he takes care of the condom and buttons his pants.

When I open my eyes again, he's next to me on the

wall, and there's a tightness in his jaw as he gazes out over the city.

"What is it?" I ask.

He takes a moment before responding. His eyes meet mine. "Was that our last time?"

I don't want it to be. I catch myself before saying it. I've let myself fall into this for the last hour, but is any of it real? All the same problems remain. What if he and I—

He nudges my shoulder. "I can see you having some sort of internal debate. Just tell me what you're thinking."

I tug at the sleeve of his T-shirt, which has ridden up over his biceps, buying time. "It's scary, though," I whisper.

One corner of his mouth turns up. "It's scary for me too." Then he takes my hand in his, interlacing our fingers.

"I really like you," I say, resigned. "Like, a lot." He waits for me to go on. "But if you hadn't cut things off, I was going to. Because the more I see you, the more I like you. And that's not good."

"I thought I was the only one." His voice is even, and now I wait for him to say more. "I was falling so hard for you, but I didn't think you felt the same way."

I crinkle my brow and smile at him. "That's so dumb."

"Well, I mean, you didn't say otherwise."

"Neither did you."

He smirks. "Fair." He lifts an arm for me, and I turn into his body, letting my face rest on his chest and neck. We hold each other tightly as the sounds of the party—Rebecca's full-body laugh and '90s R&B—drift

over us. "I wish we'd just been honest with each other," he says.

I look down at our feet, unsure. "Would that have made it any easier?"

"I think so." He sweeps my hair over my shoulder. "You don't?"

I take a breath as my mind starts to spin again. "I mean, the last two weeks have been shit. And I think you're right that not knowing how each other felt made it worse. But now that we *do* know where we are . . ."

"You still think we should end this?"

I should tell him *of course I do.* That this is never lasting.

I nestle deeper into his chest, not wanting to see his face. "Trying to get over you has really sucked. I don't know. It feels like more time together just means extending . . . that." I avoid using the word *heartbreak*, scared to reveal the true depth of my feelings.

James runs a hand up and down my arm as he thinks. If he agrees that it's best for us to go our separate ways, there's a decent chance I'll start sobbing.

"Here's the thing," he finally says, his voice deeper and more somber than usual. "We have to say goodbye in two weeks no matter what, and that's going to suck, no matter what. So." He pauses, and I wonder if he can feel my heart pounding. "Why not hold off the pain for a few more weeks?"

I want that so badly, it's frightening. "Don't we then make it that much worse?"

"Maybe," he says, calm and even. "But couldn't we also make it *better* by ending on good terms? Our own terms?"

I suspect that's not right. But I want to be hopeful. "Maybe."

He leans back, lifting my face to meet his. I have no idea if this is the correct decision, but I also know that I've already decided.

XV

JAMES

We head back to the party, and it seems no one suspected what we were up to at the other end of the roof. That is, until Lucy and I return to the dance floor and her underwear slips out of my pocket and falls to the ground. A guy in his forties drinking a margarita and dancing with mostly his neck casually picks them up and hands them to me like they're my keys. "You dropped this," he says.

"Thank you," I reply as politely as I can, the blood rushing to my ears, and when I turn back to Lucy, she's cracking up. So I present them to her in an attempt to turn the tables, but she's just as chill as he was. She makes a show of carefully folding them and placing them in her purse.

Lucy catches up with Delia before Delia leaves with Asher. Then Rebecca, Lucy, and I hit the karaoke machine for an off-key but heartfelt rendition of "Wrecking Ball" by Miley Cyrus.

When Rebecca's more inebriated friends start careening down the Slip 'N Slide, Lucy and I creep down to Rebecca's apartment, steal blankets and pillows from everywhere we can find them, curse Rebecca's too-short love seats, and curl up on the floor to sleep. The vinyl planks are hard, but Lucy's body against mine is warm and soft. Her ass presses into my thigh, and I sleep like the dead.

LUCY

The day after, I take James to lunch in my dining hall, and we both eat like we haven't eaten in days. He's in sweats he borrowed from me after our shower at my place—they're purple and too tight across his thighs, and he looks fucking adorable in them. I'm in gym shorts and the Miss Piggy T-shirt I told him about. There's a sort of freeness between us that I think comes with knowing exactly where we stand with each other.

At one point, I call something Capraesque, and James asks me what that means. I realize how much I love this about him: that he's curious and he doesn't pretend. Turns out, he doesn't know Frank Capra by name, but he knows a bunch of his movies, and we end up debating whether *Mr. Smith Goes to Washington* is too hopeful for modern audiences. I say yes; he says I should watch it again and try not to cry.

He tells me how his parents forced him to stop playing soccer in high school after he got a concussion, even though he could have gotten a scholarship. How he was so mad at them at the time, but now he sees it as an act of love.

I tell him about Delia, how she was the first friend who

made a real effort to stay connected with me whenever I traveled with my mom. She bought us matching Lisa Frank stationery to write letters and helped me believe I was someone worth holding on to.

But talk of leaving leads us back to our inevitable end and the things other than distance that would break us apart.

"I hate traveling," he says with a charming, sheepish grin.

I point at him, triumphant. "I knew it!"

He shakes his head. "I'm sorry! I know you love it, but it's just not for me."

"You don't like seeing new parts of the world? Experiencing different cultures? The *food*?"

"That's the *promise* of travel. But for me, it's just been a lot of time and money and inconvenience for something that's usually a letdown."

I want to understand him, not just cement why we're essentially opposites. But my experience has been so different. "Visiting new places makes me see possibility. Potential," I tell him. "It's what made me want to do what I do. Just the idea that so many nations can function so differently from one another, and yet they mostly function. The entire *concept* of international law is a fucking miracle."

His smile is so big that it makes me blush.

"I just really like knowing what's coming." His tone is unapologetic, confident. "Waking up in the same comfortable bed. Going to the same familiar places. Always having friends and family around. I don't know. I like feeling grounded."

I run a finger up and down his forearm. "Sounds like you want to be a plant."

"Yes. Ideally a fern." I grin, and he leans over the table, his eyes brightening. "Admit it. That sort of life would drive you insane."

I lean in to match him, our noses a few inches apart. "It sounds like fucking torture."

James sits back and chuckles.

"*I* love waking up somewhere new and knowing the day is going to be an adventure, that I'm going to learn something or see something I've never seen before." I point a stern finger at him, making him crack a smile. "*But*. That doesn't mean hitting every item on some tourist checklist. You can't *try* to make unforgettable memories. My mom taught me to look at it more like, 'Hey, today is Tuesday. How can I make this Tuesday different from the last one?'"

James gazes at me like I've almost convinced him. "You know today is Sunday, right?"

I throw a napkin at him, and we both laugh.

JAMES

After lunch, Lucy has an hours-long bar exam study session, and I have a catering gig, but we plan to meet back up for a late dinner at my place. I make us Gruyère-Fontina grilled cheeses, and she sleeps over. The next night we go see the one-woman mermaid show my roommates are producing, and it's actually kind of amazing. I sleep at Lucy's place that night, and then again the night after that.

In bed, I tell her about the restaurant plans that are coming together: the contractor I found and the replacement for the paisley wallpaper. I don't tell her I'm excited to get to Oregon to start work in earnest.

She shares how anxious she is about the bar exam and how much *more* anxious she is about the grant, even though her advisor told her he'd be "shocked to death" if they didn't select her. I don't know what she isn't sharing with me, and I try not to notice the cloud looming over us in the quietest moments.

If I thought there was even a chance of us turning this into something real, I'd tell her I love her. But what would be the point?

I'm on the subway, heading back to my place from Lucy's, repeating what's become a mantra: *This is going to end. That's just the way it is.*

My phone vibrates. I've barely thought about another living person for the last four days, so it's jarring to see Miriam's name pop up on my screen.

"Hey you," her text reads, "I heard from Dave that you're moving back to Newport to open a restaurant. Is that true?"

I almost forgot that I was planning to reach out to Miriam when I move back. Definitely not yet. Just getting this message feels disloyal to Lucy.

And contacting me with a “Hey you” . . . that has certain implications. This doesn’t feel like a friendly check-in.

I do want to see Miriam in Oregon. She’s someone who makes sense for me. And I think I make sense for her. I don’t want to deal with this now, but I don’t want to leave her waiting.

After opening and closing the message a few times, I start typing, “that’s the plan. how’ve you been?”

Then I take out my notebook and jot down tweaks to the fresh-pea risotto I’m going to menu test for Lucy tonight.

XVI

LUCY

This morning, before we part ways for long workdays, we get bagels, and he scribbles a rose onto the back of the receipt. It's so beautiful, the lines so confident and practiced, that I feel the urge to frame it. I imagine a whole wall filled with my favorite James sketches, each carefully encased and arranged by me.

And then I remember that I don't frame things. My mom taught me that. Frames are a bitch to pack. "Keep your memories with you, but keep them light," she'd say.

He tosses the rose—which maybe he thinks of as just a receipt—in the trash as we leave the shop, and I don't stop him.

As I head home to spend hours with tort law, I need distraction. I should be hearing back about my grant application any day now. And I'm damn-near positive that what I feel for James is love.

I search for new things about him that are turn-offs. He hates traveling, and he has this green shirt that I dislike. Then I start to struggle.

It sounds like he got fired from his last real job in Philly? I'm not sure, but that's the way he made it sound the night we met, and he's barely talked about that restaurant since. Maybe because he's embarrassed? It's hard to imagine anyone firing James—his food is heartbreakingly good—but maybe that says something about his work ethic or, I don't know, his professionalism? Something about it doesn't add up.

My eyes are on the ceiling as I brush my teeth. He'll be back tonight, then we're meeting Rebecca for brunch in the morning. I resist the urge to count the number of sleepovers remaining before I leave.

I trudge back into my room and collapse onto my bed. A small part of me is looking forward to the end. The last week has felt like limbo. I want to get unstuck, muscle my way through the awfulness, and move forward with my life.

I grab my laptop off my desk and pull it onto my stomach to start today's study session. The bar exam is over a month away, but all this time with James has put me woefully behind.

My heart stops when I see my inbox.

I have two new emails. One from the law firm I'm hoping will make me an offer, and one from the administrators of the grant.

Neither subject line gives any hints about the contents, and I waffle for a minute, my heart now pounding, trying to decide which to open first.

The law firm. That feels more likely to contain good news.

As my eyes quickly scan the letter, I breathe a sigh of relief—phrases like "congratulations" and "we'd love to have you" jump out at me. Then I make myself calm down and actually read the whole thing.

They're making me an offer, like I thought they would. The starting salary is frankly absurd—more money than my mom made in five years, even at the height of her makeup career. They assume I'd like to be based out of the New York office, but they'd be happy to have me in Chicago or Portland. And they'd like me to get back to them with my decision by the end of next week.

Fuck.

This should feel good. But the fact that I immediately imagine what it would be like to move to Portland—and thus be within driving distance of James—makes my heart clench and my stomach drop. I never would have even *considered* Portland five weeks ago.

But this is just my backup, I remind myself. This firm doesn't know I've landed the UN International Court of Justice clerkship. If I get the grant, I can defer this offer and decide where to move once my stint there is done.

My hands start shaking as I hover over the grant email. I don't know when it happened, but I'm sitting up in bed now, trying to take deep, slow breaths—and failing pretty miserably. I shake my head and remind myself that my advisor said I was a lock. They always give it to people in my situation. I've got this. Everything is going to work out.

I click on the email but squeeze my eyes shut before it pops onto my screen. *Why am I so scared?* I force myself to read the first few sentences, and I feel the blood drain from my face.

"We are deeply impressed by your application, your credentials, and your commitment to the foundation's mission," it says, "but unfortunately, due to unforeseen financial shortfalls, we will not be able to fund this grant for the foreseeable future."

I didn't get it. No one got it.

It vanished.

This wasn't supposed to happen.

How am I going to pay for an apartment? How am I going to feed myself?

My chest starts to heave as it sinks in that I may not be going to The Hague after all. My big plan is crumbling before my eyes.

And the next thought I have . . . is Portland.

My head suddenly feels like it's being smashed with a vise grip. I lean over just in time to throw up into my trash can.

That miserable feeling I had when I was trying to quit James cold turkey—this is worse. Just the idea of letting go of this dream position over something as stupid as money and settling for a job in a city I know nothing about, could actually hate, to be close to a guy I've known for a few weeks? It makes me feel disgusting.

People change their life plans for love all the time. They give up opportunities, make sacrifices. At least that's what I hear. But this isn't about making concessions. We want opposite lives. I want to be a citizen of the world, and he wants to be a fern. Am I supposed to give up my entire life plan to go sit on a balcony in Oregon?!

I can't. I won't.

And yet.

If I'm being really honest . . . a tiny part of me wants to do exactly that.

Fuck.

I can't tell James about the law firm offer. Or about not getting the grant. Not until I figure out what I'm going to do. On my own.

There has to be something I'm missing. Some way to make this work. But it's hard to imagine what that could be as I hobble to the bathroom to rebrush my teeth. I feel like my brain is shaking inside my skull.

I'll talk to my advisor. Reach out to the team at the ICJ. Maybe there are some secret funds somewhere that can help me? Maybe I can take out a loan?

The winterfresh paste is too bright on my brush, sickeningly upbeat. As I spit, the tears come. *I wish my mom were here.*

I steady myself by pressing my palms into the cold bathroom counter, digging into it with the pads of my fingers.

If I have to let the clerkship go and take this job instead, I'll stay in New York. That's the only sensible thing to do. I have to make this choice for myself alone. I won't be able to look at myself otherwise.

I am not fucking up my future for a guy. I won't make my life small.

Frankly, I'm better than that.

XVII

LUCY

The brunch spot Rebecca picked is an Aussie place near her apartment with cheap mimosas and big breakfast sandwiches. James and I walk to the restaurant from my place, and I know I'm acting weird—I keep dropping his hand to mess with my hair—but I can't tell if he notices.

Last night I was sure I was going to either spill my guts about the job offer and grant failure or be super awkward and suspicious all night. So I preempted both of those outcomes by spending too much money on a fifth of Angel's Envy and drinking a few fingers before James even arrived. We ended up getting drunk, watching *Top Gun*, and falling asleep without having sex. It was a huge success.

But now that we're both sober, I can feel the withheld information biting at the back of my throat, wanting to come out.

It would be cruel to get his hopes up about Portland—which I'm not even considering anyway—and I really don't need to add guilt from him to my mixed bag of emotions at the moment. So for now, we walk in silence.

JAMES

Lucy is being weird. She was last night too, with the whiskey, like she was performing or something. Now she just seems nervous.

Or maybe she's reacting to *my* weirdness. I haven't told her that I've been texting with Miriam. It's nothing of substance: She sent me a photo of her new haircut. I sent her back a picture of a chair I'm considering for the restaurant.

I keep reminding myself that I'm not doing anything wrong. But the pit in my stomach disagrees.

I thought I was doing a decent job acting like myself over the last few days, but maybe Lucy has picked up that something is different. Our vibe is clearly off. Which makes this the absolute worst time to go to brunch with Rebecca.

Rebecca, the bloodhound who can sniff trouble from miles away and never fails to call it out.

LUCY

We snag the last open table wedged among a dozen others on the restaurant's patio. Rebecca hasn't arrived yet, and I need her to. A gangly waiter about our age approaches as soon as we sit and hands us menus. "Get you started with something?"

"We'll do the carafe of mimosa, please," I say.

James gives me a little look. "Really?"

I feel my cheeks warm. "What?"

He shakes his head, looking a little embarrassed himself. "Sorry. Just after all that whiskey last night."

"It's brunch," I say, as if that's a defense.

"No, you're right." He turns to the waiter. "I'll just have a coffee. Thank you."

Now my cheeks are burning. I know I should let it go, but—"You're going to make me drink alone?"

James scrunches his brow. I can see his defenses going up, the flex of his neck muscles. "I'm not making you do anything. I bet Rebecca will drink with you."

"That she will," Rebecca proclaims, striding up to the table. *Thank god.* She plops into her chair and looks from my face to James's and back again. "What did I miss?"

I smile sweetly. "James just thinks I'm an alcoholic."

James flinches. He leans toward me with a concerned—maybe slightly annoyed—expression. "Are you OK?"

I shrug my shoulders, like he's the one being odd. "It was a joke."

I feel Rebecca looking between us again as I pick up my menu and focus on it like it's the most important legal document I've ever read.

"You two have a good week?" she asks, her tone cautious.

I shoot her a tight-lipped smile in response, trying to seem normal.

"Yeah, very good." He smirks, then shrugs. "Sorry. You just caught our first fight."

Rebecca laughs, and the sound of it—plus James's apparent ease—helps me emotionally reset. "You call that a fight?" she asks. "You guys are amateurs!"

Stop being weird. Just breathe.

I reach under the table and squeeze James's hand—an act of contrition. He squeezes back.

JAMES

Grateful that we're all ready to move past whatever that was, I settle into my chair.

Rebecca reaches a hand out to touch Lucy's arm. "How are you doing today?" There's an unusual softness in Rebecca's voice.

Lucy also seems thrown by the tone of the inquiry. "I'm fine?"

Rebecca stares at Lucy, and I try to figure out what the hell is happening right now. Rebecca seems to know something I don't—and maybe that Lucy doesn't either.

Rebecca draws an invisible circle around her own face with her finger. "I thought you'd be a bit more . . . dolled up."

"Rude," Lucy immediately responds. Then her shoulders fall. Her face turns gray. "Oh my god."

"What?" I put a hand on the small of her back. "What am I missing?"

Rebecca keeps her focus on Lucy. "It's OK. It's still early in the day. You didn't miss it."

"But I forgot it was even coming up!"

"You've had a lot going on. Don't beat yourself up."

"Can someone please fill me in?" I interject again,

which feels disrespectful, but I also feel like I don't know something important and am letting Lucy down.

Rebecca bites her bottom lip. "It's her mom's birthday."

Oh. Fuck.

Lucy presses the heels of her hands to her forehead and stares down at the table, unable to meet our eyes. "I've had this tradition since she died of doing my makeup super glam on her birthday, using all the tools I inherited from her, trying to re-create some of the looks she taught me."

Rebecca leans toward me. "She's got this amazing case of brushes and palettes. It's insane."

My mind jumps to Lucy's room. The only makeup I remember is the mascara she keeps on her bathroom counter.

Then I remember the metal trunk on wheels that lives in the corner. I've never asked about it or seen it open. I always assumed it held winter clothes.

I find myself suddenly hurt that she never showed it to me.

I realize that Lucy and Rebecca are still talking and tune back into the conversation. Lucy is still upset, but she's calming down. "Maybe later I can try some of her prosthetics," she murmurs, her brow furrowed. "Because she didn't only do editorial makeup."

"I've seen the photos," Rebecca says with an encouraging smile. "Your mom was legit."

"Why haven't you shown me any photos?" I ask without thinking. I can hear the upset in my voice. It's muted, but it's there. I try to counteract it with a shrug.

Lucy stares at me with sharp eyes for a moment. "Why would I?"

I feel the anger rising in my throat. Maybe she meant "I didn't think to show you" or "There wasn't really a good time." But that's not what she said. Her words imply that I have no business learning anything real about her. That I am a memento of her time in New York at best.

And I suppose I am.

I exhale audibly. "You're right. You wouldn't."

I drop my gaze to my menu without actually reading it, and I feel Lucy's black eyes burning into me. Seems I hit a nerve.

Good.

The waiter walks up with my coffee, two champagne flutes, and the carafe of mimosa.

"Are we ready to order?" he asks politely.

Rebecca gives him a big, plastered-on smile. "I think we're going to need another minute."

The three of us sit in tense silence, and Rebecca busies herself filling the glasses. Lucy takes a big gulp from hers. I let my coffee burn my tongue.

LUCY

I drink my drink and stew, deeply upset at James for being so deeply upset at me. He just heard what a hard day this is. Am I in trouble now for, what, not sharing my grieving process with him? That's pretty fucked.

"James, when is your flight?" Rebecca asks, and I can tell she's trying her best to reset the mood.

"Week from Monday," he responds dryly. "The day after Lucy's."

"Are you excited to get back to Oregon?"

"I am," he says, and I know he means it. It hurts my pride—even though a few days ago I was equally amped about The Hague. Now all I feel is dread. And anger.

"I'm excited for the restaurant," he goes on. "Being near family again."

"Ahem," Rebecca says.

"Inferior family," he concedes, and Rebecca grins. I silently curse both of them for bantering when I'm this pissed.

"And I'm excited to reconnect with old friends," James adds.

His eyes flick to me on the word "friends," and something about the way he says it gets under my skin. He's mentioned a few childhood friends he's still close with, but who would merit that look?

Rebecca has evidently caught something too. "Miriam's not still there, is she?"

Who the fuck is Miriam?

JAMES

"She is there, I think." Why did I add the *I think*? Coward. And why did I bring up old friends at all, like I was fishing for this question? Like I was hoping to make Lucy jealous?

Well, it's done now. Change the fucking subject, quick. "Does anyone want to split the breakfast pizza?"

"Who's Miriam." Lucy says it more as a statement than a question. She's staring at me, her eyes like daggers.

I meet her gaze. "Just an old girlfriend." I try to keep my voice neutral, pushing any vestiges of upset to the side.

Lucy's attention drops to her menu. I think for a second that she might let it go. "You've never mentioned a Miriam."

Rebecca flashes me a look of apology as she takes a big gulp of her mimosa. But maybe this is good. I set aside my feelings of guilt over Miriam, and indignation takes over.

"No, maybe not."

"Why?"

I smile at Lucy to cover just how angry I feel. "Really?"

"What?"

"You're upset with me for not telling you about one girlfriend when you've told me basically nothing about yourself?"

"That's not true—"

My brain is on fire, and I can't keep myself from carefully enumerating the omissions. "The *first* night we met you told me about your mom. Barely a word since. I only know where you've been from the posters on your walls. Basically no stories from your childhood. I don't know if you want kids or how you got interested in law—"

"Jesus, all right, I get it. Forgive me for not boring you with a bunch of biographical details that *don't matter*."

"They matter to me."

"Well, they shouldn't."

I nod, furious. "Right, because we're just . . . whatever the fuck this is. You'd never *actually* be with someone like me."

Lucy looks genuinely taken aback. "What is that supposed to mean?"

"Forget it."

"No, tell me what you mean. You think I'm some kind of snob? That I look down on you?"

"Well, don't you? I'm just a cook from a small town."

"You're a chef."

The way she says "chef" pisses me off even more. "That's a bougie word for cook. Hell, you do it with your mom too. Any time her being a makeup artist comes up, you qualify it with 'she was one of the best' or 'her work was very high end.' Who fucking cares? Why can't she just be a makeup artist? Why does that embarrass you? Why does her life have to be big and important to matter?"

A crinkle appears between Lucy's brows. "How dare you talk about my mother." Her voice is low and quiet.

"One of us should."

I've gone too far and I know it. My anger that was so hot a moment ago is devolving into shame. She doesn't deserve me coming at her like this. Especially not today.

My eyes are on my lap. I don't want to face Rebecca,

who I've never known to be this silent. And I certainly don't want to face Lucy. But I have to. I raise my head to apologize to her.

But she's already getting up and walking out of the restaurant.

"Shit." Rebecca's watching me with a look that's half pity, half judgment. "You really love her."

There it is. The truth I've been hiding from. That I hoped no one else could see. I'm not sure what to say or do.

Rebecca throws up her hands. "Go after her, dummy."

I squeeze her shoulder as I jump up and run out the door.

LUCY

I can barely see through my tears as I hurry down the sidewalk, away from the restaurant. I'm not sobbing. I'm not making a sound. My main emotion is fury.

Fury and heartbreak.

How could James think those things about me? How could he—

Fine. Maybe I've diminished him in my mind, tried to keep him at a distance. But that was self-preservation. I never did or said anything to make him feel less than.

Did I?

And my mom *was* a fucking great makeup artist, and I will always be extremely proud of her, so fuck him all the way to hell for saying—

"Lucy!"

James is running down the street after me, already starting to sweat. I don't stop, but he catches up and starts walking alongside me, giving me a few feet of space. "I'm sorry." He stuffs his hands in his pockets, as if to keep himself from reaching out. "That was fucked up, what I said back there. I know how much you love your mom and how much you admire her. I'm really sorry."

I hate that he sees the tears rolling down my face right now, but I'm too proud to wipe them. I don't want to even look at him. "I don't think you're not good enough for me."

He hesitates. "OK."

That pisses me off. I stop and turn on him. "I don't!"

James's eyes are wide and soft. "I believe you. I just—" He pauses again. "*I* don't think I'm good enough for you." He shakes his head. "I don't know why I put that on you."

I glare at him, now mad at him for a new reason. "Well, you are."

He gives me a tiny, sad smile. "OK."

We stand in silence for a moment, staring at each other. I'm still crying, and I'm not sure how to stop.

"I really am sorry," he says again. "I feel like something has been off between us since last night. And I don't know how to fix it."

Clearly, I've done a fucking terrible job keeping my shit together since getting the news about the job offer and the grant. But I still don't want to tell him either of those things. "There's nothing to fix."

I can't keep doing this. What's the point? Why am I torturing myself—and apparently him—this way? This was only ever going to end badly.

I take a deep breath. "Maybe it's just time for this to be over."

James's shoulders sink, and his hands come out of his pockets. "I don't want that." He closes the gap between us and takes my hands in his. Knowing this might be the last touch I ever get from him makes his fingers burn in mine. "I'm not ready for this to end."

I pull a hand away to wipe my tears and feel him squeeze the other, unwilling to let it go. I know what I need to do. "It already has ended."

"Lucy." James seems unsure what to say, and I don't want to say anything. I want to be done.

"Take care of yourself," I mutter. I free my hand from his, take one final look at him, and turn and walk away.

This time, he doesn't follow.

XVIII

LUCY

I walk home in a daze, and a few hours later, I manage to get it together enough to call my advisor, but he's in the Middle East and unreachable for the next week. So next I email the clerkship coordinator at the International Court of Justice to explain my situation and see if they have any way to help. The answer is a very apologetic but firm no. The coordinator asks if they should remove me from the register, and I actually scream "No!" at my computer before quickly typing a measured response. I'll figure it out. Somehow. I'll figure it out.

But it's Tuesday now, and I haven't figured it out. I'm unshowered, in the same tank top and gym shorts I threw on when I got back from brunch. It's been three days of sobbing interspersed with *Golden Girls*.

I've never felt this hollow. I'm heartbroken about James. I'm terrified about my work situation. All I want to do is call my mom and work through it with her, and I can't.

There's no one I really feel like I can talk to about all this. Rebecca's been texting me multiple times a day to check in, but I've only managed to send back the briefest of responses, mostly to let her know I'm alive and don't want her to come over.

If I tell her about the work stuff, I'm 98 percent confident she would insist on lending me the money to go to The Hague. She's about to be making bank as a first-year associate in Big Law. It wouldn't be *easy*—she's got student loans plus the cost of living in New York—but I'm almost certain she'd offer to float me what I need for the next ten months and say I could pay her back when I start getting my own paychecks.

My rational brain tries to convince me that's a good option. But I want to throw up every time I seriously contemplate it. That would be a *massive* loan. It's too much strain on our friendship. It would change the dynamic, and I couldn't put her out like that.

Not to mention that I would feel like total shit for relying on her in that way.

The best option at the moment is to stay in New York and take the job here. I can do that. I don't *want* to do that. But I can.

It just feels like admitting defeat. Like I'd be starting my career from a place of fear. I'm supposed to be out there taking on the world. Instead, I might end up stuck in place, missing out on the first big opportunity that has come my way.

A sought-after law job in New York is not the end of the world. I know that.

I just can't fight the feeling that it could very well be

the first big concession of many. It's like I have this dream of who I can be if I stand firm and stay true to myself, but life is holding up a chisel to it, and the chips are already starting to fly.

And the really scary part? There's a part of me that still, even now, wonders what it would be like to hand the chisel over to James. To see how it would feel to settle into his life and his seaside plans. Maybe it wouldn't drive me insane. Maybe the love I feel for him could completely make up for all the parts of me I would have to abandon to stay in his life.

God, I miss him.

I queue up another season of *Golden Girls*, painfully aware that even this show will come to an end.

JAMES

I've called Lucy eight times, but she hasn't answered. I started walking toward her building yesterday after a gig, but then I felt creepy and turned around. If she doesn't want to see me, I shouldn't force it.

Miriam texted me a recipe she thought I'd like a few days ago. I haven't responded. I don't have any mental space for her right now.

All I have space for is checking for a missed call from Lucy and counting down the days on my calendar. It's Wednesday now. She's leaving on Sunday, and I fly out Monday. In theory, we could have *at most* a few more days together. So what am I fighting for? What am I trying to hold on to?

I have the day off, and I should be doing something productive. But I spend all afternoon wallowing around my apartment, feeling like an idiot. I really fucked up at brunch, I know that. But before we had our fight, something was already bothering her. Pulling her away from me. I replay it again and again in my head while I stare at bedroom walls that won't be mine in a week.

Rebecca shows up with Szechuan takeout around 6 p.m. under the auspices of "helping me pack," even though I only have two duffel bags with me in New York. Most of my stuff is in a shipping pod currently on its way from Philly to Oregon. She gives me a big hug and asks how I've been. I suppose I could soften it, but "Total shit" is what comes out.

Rebecca smiles and nods. "Sounds about right."

I lead her into the kitchen, and we start unboxing mapo tofu and cumin lamb. My two French roommates walk through and eye Rebecca with extreme levels of suspicion. "This is my cousin, Rebecca."

The relief on their faces is immediate as they scamper over to double kiss her. "Oh, la cousine!" Chloe chirps. "We think he try to replace his love so fast!"

Rebecca laughs and takes their outstretched hands—they're very touchy. "No, no!" Rebecca laughs. "Lucy is actually my best friend. I introduced them."

"This is wonderful!" Alba coos. "Then you can bring zem back together!"

"Zey were so cute. And very discreet lovers." Chloe winks at me. "But we always knew."

"OK," I interject. "That's enough of that." My roommates fawn over Rebecca's "mermaid hair" for another minute before leaving us in peace.

"I like them." Rebecca opens cabinets looking for plates. "And I take it they like Lucy."

"Everyone likes Lucy," I reply without thinking and feel my ears heat. I pick up a carton of string beans in an attempt to eat my feelings.

Rebecca is quiet for a moment. "Have you two talked?"

I shake my head. "I've called. A lot. No response."

She sighs. "So that's just it?"

"I guess so."

When I look up, Rebecca is crying over her plate. "Rebecca . . ."

"I'm sorry," she moans, wiping her tears. "I'm just so fucking *bummed*." I grin at that, and it makes Rebecca laugh. She blots her eyes with thin takeout napkins. "I know this was never supposed to be a real thing, but you two fucking *fell* for each other—"

"I fell for her."

Rebecca glares at me. "Dude. You know that girl loves you."

I shake my head. "I don't know that. I thought she might for a minute, but clearly I was wrong."

"Why clearly?"

My skin feels hot as the scene replays for the thousandth

time. "You saw that fight. She kept me at a distance all summer."

Rebecca frowns. "If anything, I think her feelings for you might be more intense than yours."

I laugh at that and cross my arms, but Rebecca's expression is dead serious.

"You've known all sorts of love in your life," she goes on. "Including Miriam." Rebecca sets down her chopsticks to underscore her point. "All Lucy ever had was her mom. She's lived this big, adventurous life, but she's never been in love before. Not *romantic* love. I obviously love her more than any man ever will." She smirks. "But you're the first person she's really fallen for. And I bet you anything that has her *terrified*."

I want to write off Rebecca's words as empty platitudes, but this would be an insane way for her to go about making me feel better. "You haven't talked to her?" I ask.

Rebecca shakes her head. "All she'll say is that she's fine and doesn't want to get into it." The corners of her mouth go up, but her eyes are still sad. "I've never really known her to be one to talk through her emotions. She honestly scared the shit out of me on graduation day with her bathroom breakdown." Rebecca's face falls. "Please tell me you already knew about that."

I can't help smiling at the memory as I stab at a piece of lamb. "We talked about it that night. It was the most open she ever was with me." I realize something, and it makes my throat tighten. "Maybe I've been chasing the memory of that night ever since."

Rebecca presses her fingers to her temple, like she isn't sure what to say.

I shake my head, my eyes on the floor. "I just wish I knew if any of it was real. I mean, we agreed it would be casual, but I don't think it ever was. Not for me, at least." My brow furrows as I try to work it through. "Why would she push me away so suddenly? I was a dick at brunch, but she kinda was too." Rebecca tilts her head in tacit agreement. "Something was off with her, and I just don't know—"

I freeze mid-bite.

Her application. She'd been waiting to hear back. She should have heard by now. "Did Lucy tell you whether or not she got her grant?"

Rebecca's face falls. "Oh, shit."

I grab my phone and keys and bolt for the door. "I've gotta—"

"Go!" Rebecca calls after me. "I love you!"

"Love you too!" I shout as I hurtle down the stairs.

XIX

LUCY

Today, I managed to take a shower, order a pizza, and watch twelve episodes of *Gilmore Girls*. That's progress.

The law firm wants to hear my answer by tomorrow, and I've tried working up the will to call, but I'm not there yet.

I also haven't gotten up the nerve to tell my clerkship that I won't be showing up. Or to call the airline to try and beg for a refund for my nonrefundable Netherlands ticket.

It's almost 7 p.m., and I realize James hasn't reached out today. Yesterday he called three times and texted twice.

I don't want to explain myself to him, but the more time that passes, the more I just want him to hold me and tell me it will be OK.

And then I want him to keep holding me.

But I know I can't have that. So I turn my mind off and my TV on.

In the midst of Emily Gilmore being iconic, my phone vibrates. It's a text from James. "lucy," it reads, "i really think we should talk. i'm in front of your building." My heart skips a beat, and I see that he's still typing.

"did you get the grant?"

I'm really not sure what happens next, but without deciding to, I'm shuffling out the front door of my building in my too-warm slippers, directly into James's arms.

JAMES

Lucy doesn't say anything for a few minutes, and I don't either. We just stand under the awning, holding each other. I didn't get a good look at her before she sank into me, but she seems about as spent as I am.

"I didn't get it," she whispers against my shoulder and neck.

"I'm sorry," I whisper back. I want to ask when she found out, what her plan is. But I resist the urge and just keep holding her.

She nestles deeper into my neck. "I don't know what I'm going to do."

"You're going to The Hague," I tell her. "That's what you're going to do."

She shakes her head, and I can feel the doubt and sadness coursing through her. "You can get a personal loan," I go on. "Or maybe I can—"

She steps out of my arms abruptly. "You can't. This is my problem, not yours. I need to figure this out on my own."

I hesitate, but I have to ask the obvious question. "Why?"

Lucy doesn't seem sure how to respond. Then she

crumples into tears, and I move to hold her again, but she puts trembling hands up to stop me. "Please don't. I don't deserve this. I don't deserve you."

"What do you mean?"

She shakes her head, looking away from me. "I got a job offer. The same day I heard about the grant. It's the firm I worked at last summer, and I knew the offer was coming, but I didn't tell you because the firm has an office in Portland." I try to keep up as the story spills out of Lucy. "And you're going to be a few hours from Portland! And it would be *so easy* for me to take that job even though they have an office here in New York that would let me stay by my friends and work bigger cases, but I don't actually want to work at *either* of those places yet because I want to go to The fucking Hague and have this amazing clerkship that I'm so proud of and that I can't imagine throwing away, but I *have* to because of stupid money, which is just so *stupid*!"

Silence falls.

Then I nod. "OK. So let's get you to The Hague."

Lucy stares at me, looking a bit stunned. Her brow is furrowed, and her tears stop falling. "What?"

"I said let's get you to The Hague. There are still bank loans. We could go in the morning—"

"You—you heard what I said about Portland."

It takes me a moment to understand what she's really asking. "Yeah. You said you don't want to move there."

"But—" Her voice softens, and uncertainty creeps in. "Would you . . . *want* me to move to Portland?"

I look into her black eyes, glistening and raw. I feel no hesitation, no fear. "Lucy. I love you. I want you to have your dream."

The tears come streaming down her cheeks once more, and she falls into me. "I love you too."

XX

LUCY

A half hour later, James and I are in the dining hall, refilling bowls of cereal. We both look like shit, but I feel some tiny modicum of hope for the first time in days.

I grin at him as he spoons Frosted Flakes into his mouth. "This is, like, our special place of honesty and overeating."

James chuckles through a full mouth. "I like that. Especially the honesty part."

"Great." I lean forward. "When did you fall in love with me?"

He sets his spoon down for the first time since we arrived. "I think it honestly started the night we met."

I feel my cheeks glow. "That was a good night."

"It was." His eyes are fixed on mine. "But the first time I really thought it was love was the night you gave me the idea about opening my restaurant in the house."

I let out a guffaw. All the pieces are falling into place. "Oh my god. It was the next morning for me."

"Really?" James seems amazed.

I nod emphatically. "*That's* why you backed away. You weren't just falling for me. You'd *fallen*."

His left eyebrow arches so high it practically reaches his hairline. "Look who's talking."

I snort-laugh. "We're such cowards."

"Total cowards." He shakes his head. "I can't believe we wasted those two weeks."

"In my defense, I thought I might be mistaking the intensity of my orgasms for love."

James nearly does a spit take, both delighted and embarrassed. "That night in particular was pretty amazing," I go on, now purposefully trying to make him uncomfortable.

And it works—his ears turn red. "It was." He manages to keep his voice low and serious. "I think the art gallery wins for intensity, but that night wins for . . . feeling."

I like that.

The first night we spent together will go down as one of the most exhilarating, glorious nights of my life. But I think I might prefer this moment with him—cereal and all. Because now I know it's real. Now I know it's love.

JAMES

"In the spirit of honesty," I say, my shoulders involuntarily tensing, "I want to clear the air about Miriam."

Lucy sips her water. "Miriam, the ex you didn't tell me about?" she asks, half serious, half mocking.

"I dated her for most of high school. She's the only

person other than you that I've loved. And we broke up after I went to Philly for culinary school. Because of the distance."

Lucy takes that in, not betraying any emotion. "She's back in Newport?"

I nod.

"And she's single?" Lucy asks.

"I'm not sure. But I think so. Nothing is happening—" I quickly add. "Or has happened. She found out I was coming back through a friend and reached out."

Lucy nods. She lifts her spoon but doesn't take a bite. I can't tell what she's thinking. "So what you're saying is," she says slowly, her voice low, "bitch is trying to steal my man?" Her eyes dart up to mine, and she grins.

"You're not mad?" I ask, still a little nervous.

"I mean, no," she says, but her voice wavers. "I obviously don't *love* it." She thinks for a moment. "She reached out to you first?"

"Yes."

"Do you think you and her will . . . ?"

I try to really consider that question, and I feel Lucy tense a little as she waits. The last thing I want to do right now—in this fragile, perfect moment—is lie. "I really don't know," I admit. Then it occurs to me: "Honestly, sitting here with you, it's hard to even picture her face."

"I bet you say that to all the girls," she jokes.

"There are no other girls like you."

Lucy looks up at me, and I know she sees that I mean it.

She leans across the table, and I meet her with a kiss,

both our asses hovering awkwardly above our seats. "Thank you for telling me," she says as she sits back. "Now please don't text her again until I leave."

I laugh and nod. "Of course."

LUCY

James's admission makes me realize I have my own explaining to do. "So about the grant. And the job," I mutter as we walk across Washington Square Park back toward my place. "I really felt like I needed to figure that out myself." I avoid turning to face him.

I see James nodding in my peripheral vision. "I get that. I'm sorry I made you feel like you couldn't trust me."

I hurry to correct him. "You didn't. I just . . . didn't." I fiddle with the hem of my T-shirt. "I'm used to doing things on my own."

"What about Rebecca? Why didn't you talk to her?"

I look down at how our feet have fallen into step as I try to process this rationally. It's so much easier to think when I'm not trying to hide anything. "I was afraid she'd offer to lend me the money. I don't want to do that to her, and I don't want to do that to our friendship. Really, I don't want to do that to *myself*." I shake my head as I try to make it make sense. "Call it pride, maybe stubbornness."

"Who, you?" James teases, and I grin.

"I'm not, like, *opposed* to the idea of charity. The grant was basically going to be charity in another form. But it's always been important to me to stand on my own two feet." I slip my hand into his. "My mom always did that. Sometimes we struggled, but she always figured it out, and I always had what I needed."

James thinks that over, his gaze lifted to the swaying tulip-tree branches. "How do you know she never had help?"

The thought brings a furrow to my brow. "I . . . guess I don't," I realize. "She didn't really talk to me about money." It's an alarming thought—and also a freeing one. If she *had* taken help, I wouldn't exactly be the first person she told. She always projected strength, even when I knew she was going through a hard time. I thought that was a virtue I inherited from her, but maybe it's more complicated than that.

James turns us down Bowery, the same street he led me down the night we met.

"Where are we going?" I ask.

"To Rebecca's." He gives my hand a reassuring squeeze. "We need an expert."

Even after our talk, I'm hesitant. "What will Rebecca be able to do?"

James leans his shoulder into mine. "I don't know. But she's smart, she knows this world, and she loves you. So let's go see what she's got."

Twenty minutes later, we're in Rebecca's apartment, and she and James sit on her matching loveseats as I pace between them, unable to sit still.

I come clean about my situation. Rebecca doesn't push.

She doesn't judge. She asks follow-up questions and nods along as I give her all the information. She's perfect—like I should have known she would be. When I finish listing all the avenues I've already explored, she leans forward. "So wait, the firm doesn't know about your clerkship?"

"No. Why?"

Rebecca claps her hands on her thrifted coffee table. "That's your answer!" Rebecca is on the edge of her seat. "You're a more valuable hire if you do this clerkship. It's *in their interest* for you to go do it."

The fog in my head starts to clear, and the pieces fall into place. "I . . . oh my god."

James is leaned forward now, possibly even more amped than Rebecca. "Wait," he says. "They might actually *pay* Lucy's way?"

Rebecca holds her hands out to me, palms up, like she's serving me this idea on a platter. "They could give you an advance or some sort of loan. I mean, they *could* say no, but it really shouldn't matter to them when you start if you're off doing something that makes them look good."

I pull her off the couch and grip her in a tight hug. "Rebecca. You brilliant minx."

I feel her smile in my hair. "I *am* very minx-like."

My mind is spinning, and I'm filled with terrifyingly high levels of hope. I've been grieving the loss of my clerkship alongside the loss of James for days, and now I could have them both back. If only for a moment.

JAMES

I busy myself reheating the Szechuan leftovers Rebecca stole from my place, somehow still hungry from the stress. Rebecca and Lucy are laid out on the floor, rehearsing what Lucy should say in her voicemail to the firm's hiring attorney. I'm taking my time plating a little masterpiece of distraction when I see Lucy stand and take a deep breath, her phone in hand.

"It's time?" I ask.

She nods. "It's time."

We form a little circle. Even though it's after 10 p.m., the hiring attorney picks up. "Cassie! Hi!" Lucy's voice is unnaturally high at first, but she recovers quickly. She puts the call on speaker as she apologizes for the hour, which Cassie brushes off as no problem at all.

Then Lucy explains her situation. Rebecca keeps giving her little nods of encouragement, and I try to stay as still as possible. Cassie congratulates Lucy on the clerkship, and Lucy eloquently lays out how she'd like to complete it before starting at the firm, but the grant she was relying on fell through—

"Oh, we can handle that," Cassie cuts in, and all three of our jaws drop. We barely manage to keep our cool as Cassie goes on that she's dealt with things like this before. Without Lucy even asking, she says she can have her signing bonus in her account in a matter of days as long as Lucy commits to a two-year contract at the firm once the clerkship is done. "And if you think that won't be enough—"

"No, that should be plenty!" Lucy's eyes are shut tight as if she can't handle this much joy. As she thanks Cassie repeatedly, Rebecca does a tiny, silent toe tap dance, and I bend over and put my hands on my knees, realizing I've barely taken a breath for minutes.

They're about to hang up with promises of Docusigns and details to be worked out over email in the morning. "Just one thing," Cassie says. "Which office would you like to work in when you get back to the States?"

My heart stops. All three of us freeze.

Lucy lifts her eyes to me. For a moment, I'm stuck.

But then a smile comes to my lips. I give her a little shrug. Like: *Say the answer you want to say. The answer that's right for you.*

"The New York office," Lucy responds.

She walks around the room as she wraps up the call, which feels like it takes an eternity. When she hangs up, her arms fall heavily to her sides. I step over to her.

"I'm so happy for you."

Lucy sinks into me. "I'm feeling about eight thousand different things right now."

I hold her close, and her cheek presses into my neck. "I hope at least one of those things is *fucking ecstatic*." Her smiling eyes meet mine, and at the sound of a *pop*, we both turn.

At some point, Rebecca sneaked off and grabbed a bottle of champagne from the fridge. Pulling three stemless glasses from a cabinet, she looks over to us. "Can we *please* get drunk now?"

XXI

JAMES

After too many drinks, we spend another night on Rebecca's floor. In the morning, I make brioche French toast and fresh raspberry jam. Lucy signs her contract, and we cheer like mad.

By eleven, Lucy is dragging me to the door. Last night, I made the mistake of admitting that even though I've been in the city for nearly two months, I feel like I've hardly seen any of it. Lucy is taking it upon herself to correct that. She tells me she's my tour guide and that I'm going to like it. It's an assertion that makes me feel dread deep in my bones.

When she tells me we're on our way to one of the best views in the city, I picture the top of the Empire State Building. I'm already moaning in my head about the long line and the cramped elevator ride.

But Lucy leads us to the Steinway Tower, one of the tallest, skinniest skyscrapers in Manhattan. There's no public access, but she sleuthed out an open house for one of the building's apartments. We ride this elevator to the eighty-first floor, trying to act like we have an obscene amount of money. Once we're in the apartment, we do a terrible job keeping up the facade of potential buyers, but no one seems to care. We ogle the view from the floor-to-ceiling windows: Central Park on one side, all of downtown Manhattan on the other. I only realize my mouth is hanging open when Lucy taps my chin.

After that, she leads me to the Museum of Modern Art. I need a break, but Lucy has planned for that. Instead of shuffling from room to room, trying to see everything, whenever we find something we both love, we sit on a bench and spend time with it, taking it in silently or chatting about other things entirely. In front of Chagall's *I and the Village*, I take out my notebook and tear out a piece of paper for her. We draw for a few minutes, then she unveils her masterpiece: a stick figure goat. I reveal my sketch of her hand resting on her collarbone. She nearly gasps when she sees it, then kisses me more passionately than is appropriate for a museum. In the gift shop on the way out, she buys a thin, silver frame for my drawing.

From there she takes me to a tiny banh mi place on Fifty-Second Street she says she researched while helping me figure out my restaurant stuff. It's set up in a basement with a small, open kitchen and no space for diners, but they're making it work. We carry our sandwiches to a tiny, shaded park across the street.

"How do you do it?" I ask Lucy as she takes an exceptionally large bite.

"Do what?" she responds with a coy smile, as if she doesn't know.

"Make being a tourist not terrible." I chew and savor the perfect alchemy of crisp baguette, minced pork, and pickled cucumber. Lucy laughs. "Seriously. I'm not saying I'm totally converted or anything. But we've been on our feet for hours, we've gone multiple places, and somehow I'm not cranky or overstimulated. I feel like myself, and I don't like you any less."

Lucy laughs harder, her chin lifted to the sky, then she leans in to kiss me. "You haven't traveled until you've traveled with me, baby," she says against my mouth. "Travel doesn't need rules and expectations. You make it what you want." She smirks at me. "And go with the people you'd want to be with anyway."

I kiss her again, then we both turn back to our last few bites of banh mi. It's the kind of food I want to make—simple, accessible, and comforting. "Thank you again for your encouragement with my restaurant," I say, nudging Lucy's shoulder with my own. "The night we met, I never actually told you why I left my job in Philly." She crinkles her brow and waits for me to go on. "The head chef wanted me to be her sous. She offered to train me to take over for her in a few years, but I said no."

Lucy punches me in the arm. "You totally let me think you got fired!"

I laugh. "I mean, it kind of felt that way. That restaurant was one of the top places in the city. I honestly didn't think I could handle it, so I quit."

Lucy opens her mouth, undoubtedly to call me an idiot and compliment my cooking in the same breath, but I don't let her. "These last six weeks, though, you've helped me realize that my doubts weren't actually about my talent."

I pause to look her in the eye. "I don't *want* a Michelin star. I don't want to make food people are more excited to take pictures of than actually eat. I want to make the food *I* love, food that means something to me." I see a swell of pride in her eyes. "Now I'm going to get to do that. And I'm going to be fucking great at it."

Lucy leans over, puts her hand on my thigh, and gives me a deep kiss. "And it's all because of me," she brags.

I carefully set aside my last bite and pull her onto my lap. She squirms.

"OK! OK! You get *some* of the credit!"

Then her lips are on mine, and she presses her body tightly against me. Sliding my palm up her spine under her shirt, I try to hold on to the fact that we're in a park and I can't take all her clothes off right now. I almost forget and start to unclasp her bra as she rubs her ass into me, making me throb.

But then she pulls her lips away to make eye contact. "Come on. We've got one more stop before home."

"I think we should go home. Now."

She smirks at me, stands, and starts to walk away. "It'll be worth it."

"You're getting cocky," I call after her.

"Trust me!" she yells back. And I do.

Thirty minutes later, we're at a Chinese foot-massage parlor that I had no idea was around the corner from my rental. For a pittance, we book an hour, and any aches I gathered throughout the day fade away. I doze off in the chair, and I wake up to Lucy gently nudging me, her black eyes glowing.

"I'll go anywhere with you," I whisper, and she kisses my freckle.

LUCY

The next morning, James tells me he's taking the reins, and his plan is for us to spend the entire day on a picnic blanket in Central Park. I've never done well staying in one place for long without an agenda. Unless the *Gilmore Girls* or *Golden Girls* are involved.

But he followed my lead, and I'll follow his. I make sure my phone is fully charged for emergency doomscrolling while James fills a cooler and stuffs a backpack to the brim.

He spends a good fifteen minutes scoping out a spot for us, and I can feel my patience already waning. But when he finally spreads a blanket under a massive sycamore tree that will give us shade all day, I have to give him credit. There are no visible bugs, there's no mud, and somehow we're secluded from the walking paths, but there are still plenty of parkgoers for people watching.

I sit on the blanket, trying to convince myself that maybe this won't be so bad, and James presents me with the first item from the cooler: frozen grapes. They're *exactly* what I want. I eye James suspiciously. "How did you know?"

He smirks, the freckle under his eye teasing me.

For the first hour, I'm fidgety, messing with the loose threads of my cutoff shorts, and James keeps pulling things out of his bag of tricks to put me at ease. First it's a cushion to sit on. Then a crossword book. Then a frisbee.

By the second hour, he's given me a can of sparkling wine, a scalp massage, and a used copy of *The Giver*, my favorite book from childhood. When we've been sitting on the ground for too long, he pulls up a yoga video on his phone, and we do some stretching and make excuses to touch each other.

By the third hour, I feel like I'm starting to get it. When I start getting wiggly, I try to hear the yoga instructor's voice in my head telling me to sink in and find what feels good. I end up taking a nap and waking under the swaying limbs of the sycamore, my head nestled against James's arm as he reads Vonnegut's *Cat's Cradle*.

Later, he breaks out tea sandwiches, watermelon wedges, and a party-size bag of Cheetos. I check my phone and am completely amazed to see it's approaching 5 p.m. I hold it up to show James.

He laughs. "She *can* sit still." Then he kisses me, and I pull him in tight so he won't stop.

XXII

JAMES

We spend that night at Lucy's because there's no avoiding it anymore: Tomorrow is our last full day together, and she needs to pack. Her flight leaves at nine the following morning.

We both move like slugs, kissing and crying a little as we take down her posters. Eventually, we get two suitcases loaded up for Europe, and the rest goes into a few unwieldy boxes that we'll lug to Rebecca's apartment for storage.

But before we go, Lucy wheels her mom's massive makeup case into the center of the room. I notice a little label that reads "Property of Eva Torres" as Lucy opens up the lid, showing me its contents for the first time.

I watch her put on a full face of makeup. It's hypnotic. She talks me through each step, and I ask a lot of dumb questions, which Lucy patiently answers as she does something called contouring and mixes lipstick shades together.

Once she finishes her own face, she asks if she can do mine, and we sit cross-legged on the floor as she gives me what she calls "the effortlessly hot actor"—the sort of minimal look her mom would do for male celebrities at photoshoots. When she finishes, she holds up a hand mirror for me, and I kiss her. "We're so hot," I say.

I'm not sure I've ever heard her laugh so hard.

After that, she gets out a portfolio of her mom's work. There are glossy ads, magazine covers, black-and-white shots from newspapers, and a slew of Polaroids taken by Eva herself. Lucy leans into me as I study each one, asking when and where they were taken.

LUCY

After we drop my boxes at Rebecca's—and I give her three extremely long, extremely tight hugs—James and I take the subway back to my place. We sit in a mostly empty train car in the middle of the afternoon, our hands intertwined, our shoulders pressed together, both overly aware that the only thing left on the agenda is saying goodbye.

My heart is in my throat, and it has been all day. I'm genuinely excited to start this new chapter, to go have this adventure. But that doesn't help me handle the grief that's pressing into my body from every angle.

"I don't want to say goodbye," I whisper into James's shoulder, and he leans his head onto mine.

"I don't either." I feel his lips on my scalp, and I hurry to wipe away a tear. I really don't want to spend the rest of this day crying.

"Does it change anything?" he asks. "The fact that we're in love?"

"How so?"

"Well," he says, his voice a bit dreamy and far off, "we've never talked about the possibility of long distance."

I feel my chest tighten. "We've never even talked *labels*," I say, trying to lighten the mood with a joke.

I feel him grin. "I'm pretty sure once you say 'I love you,' the label is implied."

"Presumptuous," I tease, and he nudges my shoulder playfully.

We sit quietly for a moment. "I don't want to put any pressure on you. I've done long distance before, and it didn't work."

"Sure," I say, not knowing how else to respond. "And aren't you planning to call Miriam in a few days?" I ask, not in an accusatory way, simply matter of fact. That's the only way I know how to approach this conversation.

"I'll be sobbing into a bowl of ice cream and watching *Hello, Dolly!* on repeat in a few days," he replies. I chuckle and press more firmly into him. "Lucy, I'm not getting back together with Miriam. Breaking up with her was painful, but trying to let go of you has been fucking torture." I squeeze my eyes shut to keep the tears from falling. "I want more than a relationship that's just not hard. I want to really feel something. The way I feel with you."

There's a hint of nerves in his voice. "What if I came to see you in a few months?" he asks.

I've thought about this. But. "That's a really expensive

ticket, and a very long flight," I say quietly. "And I couldn't ask you to put your life on hold for—"

"No, I know. That's not what I'm asking." He looks for the right words. "I don't want either of us to be naive about this. I know you're going to New York when you come back. I know the life I want isn't the life you want."

A sad smile comes to my lips. "But it's not as bad as I thought it'd be."

He chuckles. "Agreed." Then he runs his fingers over mine. "I'm just saying, even if this doesn't make sense long term . . . I'd be willing to get on an extremely long flight for you."

I take a moment to wipe my cheeks. I try to memorize the feel of his fingertips on my skin. The shape of his blue-gray eyes. "I think we shouldn't make any decisions right now."

He's quiet, and I can sense the hurt there, but I try to stay strong.

"I'm not saying no. But I'm scared to hold on to this longer than we should. I'm scared we'd just be prolonging the hurt."

He furrows his brow, then the corner of his mouth lifts. "You mean the way we have since the night we met?"

I grin. "Exactly."

JAMES

We sit in silence for a few minutes, and I find myself growing frustrated. The quiet feels like wasted time, and we have so little left together.

But then I remember her mom's advice about traveling. About the trap of trying to make every experience an unforgettable one. My mind wanders back to our first electric night together. We could never have planned magic like that. But the ordinary moments we've shared since—folding laundry, window shopping for restaurant stemware, watching musicals, cooking in my overheated kitchen—I'll hold on to those just as tightly.

I kiss Lucy's temple. "Do you remember what you said, the night we met, about dating in your twenties?"

Lucy raises her brows. "That it's a waste? That we're too young and unsettled in our lives for love."

"You still think that?"

She thinks for a moment, then smirks. "I mean, kind of." We both laugh, then she grips my fingers tighter. "But I'm glad you didn't let me walk away."

LUCY

As soon as we're back in my room, James starts carefully unbuttoning my top and running his fingers over my shoulders and chest. He never meets my eye, keeping his gaze fixed on my skin, as if he's trying to memorize every curve, every crevice.

He slides off my pants and moves down my body with them, kissing my hips, my thighs, my calves. Then he stands and takes off my bra. He takes his time enveloping each of my nipples in his mouth as I run my hands through his hair. There are too many sensations, and I don't know how to keep track of them all. How to take them all with me.

He walks me backward until I feel my back press against the cold wall. He hooks his fingers into the waistband of my underwear and pulls them down, lowering onto his knees.

Then he presses his lips to my pubic bone, and my body begins to vibrate in anticipation. He lifts one of my legs onto his shoulder, and I close my eyes, pressing one hand into his free shoulder and my other into the wall behind me.

But he's still. When I look down, I see that his eyes are fixed between my thighs, hungrily taking in the sight of me. He lifts his eyes to mine. "You're beautiful."

Only then does he press his mouth to me, and I go completely weak in the knees. But James and the wall hold me up as I tremble through each fresh pulse of pleasure.

"I want to do this together," I say, and he carries me to the bed. I lie there in my sex haze as he tugs off his T-shirt with one hand and unbuttons his jeans with the other. Then he's pressing his weight onto me, a condom in place. I kiss him, and the faint taste of me is on his tongue. It makes me even hungrier for him.

I climb on top of him and guide the full length of him inside of me, the slightest bit of pain hitting me at the deepest point. I let out a little gasp and a quick laugh. "You OK?" James asks.

"It's a good pain," I whisper, and then I turn my brain off completely.

I curl my hips forward and back, pressing him into my G-spot and then releasing, again and again. I watch him smile at me with greedy eyes. I lean forward, and he licks my nipples with a firm, hot tongue as he takes control of the rhythm, still underneath me. Our lips lock, and he sits, bringing me upright with him. I wrap my legs around his back and pull my lips away to lean backward. We press into each other, our eyes dancing between each other's faces and our pulsing, connected bodies.

Breathing heavily, he licks his thumb and brings it to my clit, and I'm done for. I cry out. I moan. I probably disturb all my neighbors. But I don't care. I want to lose myself in this moment with James, to hold on to it for as long as I can.

Three Years Later

XXIII

JAMES

I think about that night often, the last night I spent with Lucy in New York.

We didn't fall asleep until almost five. We were trying to stop time, to not let the sun rise. In between the sex, we talked and talked. We took a shower. We managed to clothe ourselves long enough for a final meal at the dining hall, where Lucy showed me her favorite cereal combo—one part Golden Grahams, one part Cinnamon Toast Crunch—and I jokingly cursed her for holding out on me.

But what I return to most about that night is holding her. Our limbs tangled up in her bed. When her alarm went off in the morning, that's how we were. Her body felt like home. The place where I wanted to stay.

But finally, we had to let go.

She asked me to kiss her goodbye in front of her building. Tears streamed down her cheeks as she joked that she didn't want our last kiss to be on a subway platform that reeked of August. I asked to go with her all the way to the airport, but she shook her head. She didn't think she could handle that.

So I held her face in my hands and gave her a long, slow kiss. And then she left.

It's been three years, but that kiss is still fresh in my mind.

I'm reliving it for probably the millionth time as I trudge downstairs from the living space to the restaurant in what was once my grandmother's home. I've named it Esther, after her.

When I opened ten months after returning to Newport, I started small. A set menu and craft cocktails. When I had enough revenue to expand the kitchen, I brought in a proper sous-chef. In the summer, when I serve the full pork chop meal I made for Lucy, it sells out every night. A steady stream of tourists book in advance, but I make sure to set aside half a dozen tables for my regulars. It's the start of June, and last night, every seat on the porch was filled.

I'm heading back toward the kitchen to start the dinner prep when I hear the front door open. I turn to see a familiar silhouette in the morning light, a statuesque woman with a suitcase at her side and a bouquet of wildflowers in her hand. "Hello," she says, low and warm. "Are you open?"

I would know that body, that voice anywhere. I can't see yet, but I'm sure her black eyes are gleaming. And that the tips of my ears are red.

"We don't open for a few hours, actually," I say, keeping my tone even, professional.

"Can you make an exception? I've heard you make a mean brioche French toast."

She leaves her bag in the entry, sets the flowers on a table, and strides toward me. I shake my head. "I haven't made that one in quite a while."

As she comes closer, she traces a finger along the wall. It's lined with framed photos of us over the last three years. In front of a Ferris wheel during my autumn trip to The Hague. Lucy hugging a pile of books at Powell's on her first trip to Portland the following spring. Me learning to make udon when I joined her on a work trip to Tokyo. That was a few months after she started at the Portland office.

Then there are all the shots from the past year, when she started working remotely and moved here to Newport. Us on the upstairs balcony. My hands as I sketch her hands.

And of course, there are the travel posters—also all carefully framed. The one she bought me in The Hague has a place of honor over the fireplace.

Lucy slides into my arms, and this house feels complete once again. "I missed you," I say.

She grins. "So where are we on that French toast?"

LUCY

James gathers up ingredients around the kitchen like it's an extension of him as I put the flowers into my favorite vase—the mercury glass one his grandmother always kept full. He knows exactly where everything is and moves with a rhythm that's mesmerizing. I sit at the counter and watch him work, unable to stop smiling.

After my first month in The Hague, I accepted that missing James wasn't a fleeting feeling. I finally broke down and wrote him a short email, asking how things were going with the restaurant. That kicked off a nightly ritual. Throughout the day, I'd gather little anecdotes, moments I couldn't wait to share with him. I told him things in those emails I'd never told anyone, not even my mom. We got to know each other on a whole new level—a level I never fully allowed us to reach over our summer together, a level that somehow felt less terrifying with an ocean between us. I realized I still wasn't ready to put down roots in any one place, but he and I had taken root in each other.

After a few weeks, he told me he still desperately wanted to see me. So against my better judgment, I agreed to a visit. I showed him all my favorite local discoveries, taking care not to overwhelm him, but the best day of the trip was the one we spent entirely in bed—having sex, eating stroopwafels, watching *Singin' in the Rain*, and talking for hours on end.

Within a month of him leaving, I realized how stubborn I'd been in my resolve to end up back in New York. From Portland, I'd have opportunities to work in East Asian countries, places I'd been dying to explore. But I was clinging to New York as a sort of act of defiance, determined not to put a guy over my career. James stopped being just a guy a long time ago, though. Maybe he never was. And my career could be just as good, maybe even better, near him. My *life* would be better near him.

When I told Rebecca all this in a video chat, her expression said "no shit" before her mouth did.

He proposed the day after I moved into his grandmother's house—now our house—in Newport. He held a ring in front of my nose the moment I woke up, and I kissed him so forcefully I nearly knocked him out of bed. He planned the whole day for us—bowling at the local alley, his signature French dip for lunch, karaoke at the local dive bar. He even flew Rebecca out to celebrate. Her first topic of discussion was how to arrange the porch for a summer wedding.

We miss each other when I'm gone, but we still email every night, without fail. Things are going so well at the restaurant, but not yet to the point of him being able to step away for weeks on end, and I'm not sure he'd want to be away that long, even if he could. But not once has he asked me to turn down an assignment. And coming home to him has become my favorite part of any trip.

Sitting at the counter, I watch James whisk, and wafts of vanilla and cinnamon hit my nose. But my eyes can't resist the pull of his forearms. One hunger overcomes the other.

I slide off my stool and step behind him, wrapping my arms around his torso. I prop my chin on his shoulder. "On second thought, forget breakfast. Just take me to bed," I whisper in his ear.

James turns to me without hesitation, lifting me into his arms and carrying me out of the kitchen with a playful grin. "Welcome home."

Cheers to more Lucy and James: Read the book's epilogue to discover what's next for these two—this time, told from Rebecca's POV. Just scan below or visit 831stories.com/neverlasting.

More novellas like this one are waiting for you at 831stories.com, where we celebrate romantic fiction in all its forms. You can also dive into bonus content, products, events, and fan fiction and join our membership program to receive new releases early, get discounts across the site, and access all sorts of exclusive perks.

ACKNOWLEDGMENTS

First and foremost, thank *you*, person holding (or listening to) this book. Thank you for picking up this little love story and giving it your precious time. I'm deeply grateful for every page turned, every moment shared, and I hope Lucy and James bring some light to your life.

Thanks to everyone at 831 Stories, especially Erica and Claire for taking a chance on me and refusing to let me fuck this up. To Madison and Catherine for your care and enthusiasm. To Georgia Clark, Kelli Martin, Lindsey Weber, Sanjana Basker, and Erica for the intense mental and emotional labor you put into editing this story. I can say with absolute certainty that this book is so, so, so much better thanks to each of you.

To my fabulous team: Sean, Jon, Hope, Eni, Ori, and each of your respective assistants. Thank you for always having my back and never blinking when I say things like, "I think I'm going to write a romance novella." You've helped me fulfill so many of my creative dreams, and I know we've got a lot more dreamstuff ahead.

To my first readers: Becky, Cassie, Jessie, and Kennary. (Those names have great flow. Consider forming a band.) You each gave me wonderful feedback that made this book better, but perhaps even more importantly, you built up my confidence with your excessively kind words. Not sure I could have gotten through this without you. Thank you, thank you.

Mom, I miss you more by the day. This book would have made you blush every time you told someone about it, but you would have talked it up just the same. Love you always.

Dad, thank you for never once telling me to pick a more practical career. Please only ever read the heavily redacted copy I gave you.

Abel, you're the most deliriously wonderful thing that will ever happen to me. Being your mom fucking rocks. Now please put this book down and never read it. (*Maybe* you can read Pappy's redacted copy in ten years. We'll talk about it.)

Cassie, I want to be you when I grow up. Becky, you're an absolute miracle of a human being. I'm eternally grateful for both of you, my best friends for life.

To my friends, my family, my nephews and niece. I love you all so much. Thank you for making my life overwhelmingly full and beautiful.

And finally, to my husband. Thank you for not thinking I was crazy when, after dating three months, I told you I wanted to move with you wherever you went to law school. Thank you for proposing to me way too fast. Thank you for being the best partner and co-parent and accomplice imaginable. This life would be so much less fun without you.

ABOUT THE AUTHOR

Angela Bourassa is an award-winning screenwriter and mom. (Her son gave her a medal—it counts.) Her films include *If You Were the Last* starring Anthony Mackie and Zoë Chao and *Turn Me On* starring Bel Powley and Nick Robinson. Angela lives in San Diego with her husband, son, cat, and chickens. *Never Lasting* is her debut novella.

ALSO FROM 831 STORIES

Big Fan by Alexandra Romanoff

A high-profile scandal derailed Maya's DC career, and she's eager to fly under the radar—that is, until her former boy-band crush reaches out with a job offer.

Hardly Strangers by A.C. Robinson

One night with a rock star could upend Shera's best-laid plans, revealing how a chance encounter can rewrite a story—and change everything.

Comedic Timing by Upasna Barath

Naina is seeking a fresh start in NYC after breaking up with her girlfriend, but when she meets someone at a party, he's so offtype that her attraction to him fuels an identity crisis.

Set Piece by Lana Schwartz

When a breakout BBC star gets swarmed by fans during a night out, it's a no-nonsense bartender, CJ, who rescues him—and warms them both up for an after-hours hookup.

Square Waves by Alexandra Romanoff

The first spin-off in the *Big Fan* series, an enemies-to-lovers romance in which tabloid fodder mixes with a long-brewing rivalry as Cassidy contends with her high-school nemesis.

Exit Lane by Erika Veurink

A postcollege cross-country road trip sparks *something* between Marin and Teddy—though it's not quite clear what. Over the next eight years, they have fated encounters on multiple continents.

Grape Juice by Eliza Dumais

When Alice lands in France for a wine harvest, she's disenchanted with her life. But she soon finds something she's missing in the vineyard owner's nephew Henri, who's just as lost as she is.

Rooting Interest by Cat Disabato

When Felix gets pulled off her NFL beat to cover the WNBA, she doesn't expect to find herself so taken with the sport—or with one of its biggest stars, Natalie Czapski.

Found Time by Caroline Goldstein

Lili and Reid lock eyes after a 1993 Jeff Buckley show. Thirty years and a whole lifetime later, they cross paths once more. Can they finally make their way back to each other?

Major Gift by Tiffany Ezuma

Ndidi, the widow of a billionaire tech mogul, is determined to give her wealth away—and keep one secret from Geoffrey, the perceptive journalist tasked with telling her story.

Down to Earth by Julia Turshen

Vegetable farmer Frankie doesn't know what to make of Paige, the Brooklyn mom who's moved to her quiet upstate town. But could the attraction she's feeling grow into something more?

Double Standard by Mallory Thomas

Ana is about to film a Greek-god epic when a sighting with her co-star threatens her career. Her plan? Fake-date his stunt double, Levi, and let everyone believe *he's* who she was spotted with.

Vacation Self by Alexandra Romanoff

When Maggie, an overworked florist, flees to Vermont for some R&R, she doesn't expect to meet Jake Ramsey, a onetime hard-partying boy-bander in recovery and out of sorts.

831 STORIES BOOK CREDITS

So many people were involved in bringing this book to life. Many of their names are included here, but there would be no HEA without the passionate work of booksellers and librarians and the enthusiasm of readers. And as we all know, romance readers are the best readers.

831 Stories

Erica Cerulo, Madison Feller, Marie Joh, Catherine Krenzer, Claire Mazur, Elaine Orihuela, Angela Vang

Authors Equity

Andrea Bachofen, Rose Edwards, Carly Gorga, Sarah Christensen Fu, Becca Kadison, Deb Lewis, Madeline McIntosh, Nina von Moltke, Diana Simmons, Erin Vandeveer, Don Weisberg, Craig Young

C47 Design

Phil Chang, Haneu Kang, Jamin Lee, Naomi Otsu, Sunny Park

Editing

Sanjana Basker, Kelli Martin, Lindsey Weber

Marketing, Events, and Publicity

Emma Benshoff, Zoë Gillespie, Tara Larsen, Ashleigh Magee, Kaitlin Phillips, Riley Vaske, Kristin White

Production

Sam Martin, Scribe Inc.

Keep reading for a taste of

Exit Lane

by Erika Veurink

from 831 Stories

I

MARIN

The sun streaks in through the slivers of window on either side of the air-conditioning unit, and it takes me a few waking moments to register the arm of my longtime on-again, off-again girlfriend draped across my chest.

As I gently lift her wrist, Georgie stirs with a devilish smile, bringing me right back to earth. "It's good luck to have sex on graduation day," she hums, kissing my face, my neck, my hip as she shimmies under the covers, armed with the vibrator she left charging the night before. I close my eyes and let my head fall back, trying to be present but feeling far away. Which is actually where I want to be.

When I finish and she comes up for air, I trace a constellation of freckles across her back. "I'll miss this," she says, rolling over into a sunspot on her pilled gray duvet.

"Me too," I say, and I mean it. It's hard to believe I came to the University of Iowa hoping people would think I was straight, worried being bisexual might be some kind of disappointment. But once I settled in—once I got over the novelty of being someone other than the girl with the dead dad—it felt like space opened up for something else. The one-hour-and-fifty-five-minute drive felt far enough away from home to try on an identity that I thought might fit. Self-assured and up-for-anything Georgie, president of Chi Omega, social coordinator of the Pride Alliance Center, helped me find a rhythm, some kind of belonging. But as I kiss her goodbye, I feel a relief, an acknowledgment that my time here is over and that my real life can start.

On campus, parents are at Hy-Vee purchasing black-and-gold "Class of 2017" balloons, cases of Coors, and flimsy greeting cards to stuff with cash. My personal celebration is going to look more like driving a thousand miles and never turning back.

As I step out into the morning sun, rolling my shoulders back into a big stretch, I hear the band tuning its instruments to *Pomp and Circumstance* on the still-dewy turf of Kinnick Stadium. Beneath it, the sound of Sloane's voice as she answers my phone call: "Why are you up?" She responds with a question. Typical. I imagine her filling in the last of the Saturday crossword in pencil while sipping a responsible half cup of coffee. "God, I see you walking from the Chi O house. You think you're so original for getting laid our last morning of college." I wave to where I know my best friend is looking down from the living room we share. She's probably already dressed—like a future First Lady, as usual, a long brown ponytail hanging at the nape of her neck, as carefully constructed as the sculptures at the state fair butter-carving competition.

"Did Teddy confirm what time he could pick me up?" I ask as I cross the street.

"Yep, you're all set to leave at five."

"We can agree he's only doing this because he's desperately in love with you, right?"

She ignores me. "You don't have a car. You're both headed to New York. It just makes sense. But I *can* agree that it is remarkable that he's still willing to do this despite your unwillingness to just text him back directly to coordinate this whole thing. But I am, as ever, happy to act as your admin. I will sort of miss it when you have a real one." Ever logical, she has a way of finishing a sentence that annoys her opponents on the debate team and fills me with calm. She's the one part of my college experience I can't bear to think about leaving. Our plan is to reunite in the city eventually, but for now, we try to avoid the topic of our inevitable distance.

After our freshman year of dorm living, Sloane and I moved into a luxury building on the edge of campus. Though her parents assure me I pay half the rent, we all know my monthly check barely covers the co-op fee.

"Your gown is steamed in the bathroom," she says as soon as I step through the door and kick off my loafers. "There's extra turkey bacon in the oven. And when are you going to deal with your closet? You know, for someone who claims to love a plan . . ."

I reach for her shoulder, smiling, and pull her in for a hug. "I trust that you'll still be micromanaging my life long-distance."

I leave her to her own preparations and collapse, for the last time, onto my bed, a wrought-iron beauty I rescued from Craigslist and transformed with the aid of Sloane and a can of spray paint on the roof during finals. I only ruined one pair of pants.

I look around at everything that's still left to pack. Dad's funeral program tucked into the frame of a pink-and-black *Funny Face* poster. Macroeconomics textbooks I promised my Chi O little. A row of blue and white button-ups, some thrifted blazers. My beloved, pristine loafers, purchased after landing a competitive venture capital internship in New York. My heart rate rises in excitement as I process the gravity of the moment, and I fan my arms like a kid making a snow angel. The back of my throat goes dry, and I'm suddenly lightheaded from anticipation, hunger, or both. Today is the start of the promise I made myself when I was fifteen: that someday I would leave all of Iowa behind. I have two suitcases. Seven hours. And a triple espresso waiting for me in the kitchen.

TEDDY

"Graduation sex"—I barely get the words out, watching Emilie, an ex from freshman year, pulling on a heel at the foot of my bed—"is good sex, I mean, good luck." She smiles, grabs her keys off my dresser, and promises to add me on LinkedIn. I laugh to myself as I tug on my boxers.

After the door shuts, I know it's time to face the

inevitable: I am moving out and moving on, even if a not-insubstantial part of me wishes my life in Iowa City could last forever—the house parties, the group projects I carried mostly on my own, the late nights in the library that turned into early mornings.

When I got accepted into the NYU School of Law, I briefly but seriously considered staying at Iowa instead. After working through a robust pros/cons chart on the whiteboard in my favorite study room in the business school, I knew what I had to do. I'd go learn everything I possibly could from a new place and new people, then bring it all back home. "We'll always be here," my mom reminded me. "Now's the time to spread your wings."

My eyes drift to a stack of cards sitting on top of my dresser: one for my sister Romy, one for my parents, and one for my childhood best friend and forever accomplice Carter. Notes thanking them for their support the past four years. Proof that learning to shotgun a beer hadn't murdered my manners.

I lean onto my elbow to open the disintegrating blinds, revealing crowds ambling toward the football field. "Amateur hour," I mutter. I'd reserved tickets for my and Carter's families weeks ago and booked an eight-person reservation for late lunch in town. Our combined family dinners used to be a weekly occurrence, most Sunday nights after football games or church, and the weight of this being the last time we'd all be together for a while was palpable. It was a pressure on my chest that kept me from moving to my feet.

I check my phone, fully charged on the windowsill

where I leave it every evening, to find a drunk voicemail I convinced Carter to record for posterity at Donnelly's last night. Nostalgic already, I download it for safekeeping and scroll back to a text from Sloane, confirming plans for me to take someone named Marin with me when I depart for my drive to New York this afternoon. I hadn't planned on company, but how could I say no to the gorgeous, divinely aloof Sloane Bachman?

Three knocks interrupt thoughts of my entirely unrequited crush.

Carter. "Decent!" I shout toward the door, and he enters, balancing two sweating iced coffees in his hands and a bag of bagels under his chin.

"Ran into a very adorable ghost on the way in," he says, dropping the carbs at the foot of my bed with a tilt of his head. "Emilie? From Econ 101?" Carter's encyclopedic memory of my dating life is both endearing and creepy. Plied with enough drinks, he could recite every single one of my love interests since first grade.

I reach for my coffee with an eye roll. "I plead the fifth?"

He laughs. "You ready?"

"One sec." I text Sloane back—promptness equals points in her book—and finally bring my feet to the floor.

The ceremony is eternal, but not long enough. Our parents are waving from row 5, zooming in with their ancient iPhones, dabbing tears. A reminder that the moisture pooling in my own eyes is genetic hardwiring. After lunch, Carter and I both continue to cry in the Joseph's parking lot while our dads pretend to make small talk ten feet away and our moms hover, patting each other's shoulders and digging in their purses for another pack of tissues. Carter is headed to Reno for a top-secret engineering job, and we've spent the last four months trying to pretend like the cross-country moves we're making aren't terrifying. That we have any idea how to navigate the world without each other. We hand each other our letters. "We're so cheesy," Carter jokes, stuffing my note in his pocket. "Obviously I can't read this now. I'm really going to miss you. Promise me you won't fall in love with some Upper East Side snob and never come back?"

I laugh and hug him hard. "It's just for now. We'll get married and have kids, and our kids will get married and have kids, and we'll hardly remember this." I say it in a joking tone, but he knows that I mean it. "Promise to save a spot for me on Fifty-First Street," I add more earnestly.

The plan has always been simple: Carter would live at 441 Fifty-First Street, Des Moines, Iowa, his grandparents' former address and the site of some of our best memories, and I would live in 443 Fifty-First Street next door. But for now, it's Nevada and New York and a shared commitment to call each other every Sunday.

I pull my late grandma's 1998 LeSabre out of the parking lot. The gas light flicks on, and the check engine light follows in short order. It's fine. What matters is getting to the meeting spot on time. In all likelihood, punctuality is Sloane's love language.

When I make the turn in front of the main library, I see them: Sloane, somehow still stoic despite tears streaming down her face, hugging a woman almost a foot taller than her—dark blond, terrifying, with a cigarette dangling from her lip and an *Annie Hall* outfit hanging off her frame. Sloane's in chinos, ballet flats, and a navy-and-white striped boatneck. Are those . . . printed-out directions in her hand? Her friend looks familiar, maybe from an elective or Young Democrats or something. I squint as I approach and pull the visor down.

Now that I have a better view, I can tell that the friend is beautiful—actually, stunning—with features that look like they could slice right through me, though a little too androgynous for my personal taste. Sloane's a gin and tonic after a long day of yard work. This woman—Marin—is a Negroni after a big meeting. *Not that I've ever had a long day of yard work or a big meeting*, I think. She intimidates me even from a distance, and yet her high cheekbones and arched eyebrows make my stomach tighten in a way I recognize. As I roll to a stop at the curb, I sit up straighter, checking for remnants of lunch in my teeth and tracking the way Marin's weight shifts from her front foot to her back, how she lifts her chin while forcing a smile.

The two of them pull apart and walk toward the Buick, where I hand-crank the passenger window open. Sloane turns on a smile, a real one I think, as she angles her stretched-out arms in a sideways V like she's unveiling a work of art. "Teddy, meet Marin."

Sixteen hours. How bad could it be? I reach over to extend a hand out the window.

"Hi, Teddy," she says, eyes narrowing. "Can you open the trunk?"